T0284354

Five Nights at Freddy's™

THE WEEK BEFORE

AN INTERACTIVE NOVEL

BY

SCOTT CAWTHON

E. C. MYERS

SCHOLASTIC INC.

Special thanks to DJSterf

Copyright © 2024 by Scott Cawthon. All rights reserved.

Photo of TV static: © Klikk/Dreamstime
Stock photos © Shutterstock.com

All rights reserved. Published by Scholastic Inc., *Publishers since 1920*.
SCHOLASTIC and associated logos are trademarks and/or
registered trademarks of Scholastic Inc.

The publisher does not have any control over and does not assume
any responsibility for author or third-party websites or their content.

No part of this publication may be reproduced, stored in a retrieval
system, or transmitted in any form or by any means, electronic, mechanical,
photocopying, recording, or otherwise, without written permission of the publisher.
For information regarding permission, write to Scholastic Inc., Attention:
Permissions Department, 557 Broadway, New York, NY 10012.

ISBN 978-1-5461-3111-3
10 9 8 7 6 5 4 3 2   24 25 26 27 28

Printed in the U.S.A.   131

This edition first printing 2024 • Book design by Jeff Shake

Intro

You are Ralph, and working security at Freddy Fazbear's Pizza is your dream job—at least that's what you told them in the interview. You've been there so long, the relentlessly cheerful animatronic characters feel like old friends. You love how their antics bring saccharine smiles to kids' faces. This place creates happy family memories, and *you* help make that possible.

But all good things must come to an end—it's time to move on while you still can. This is your last week. You've always worked the day shift, but after a sudden staff vacancy and temporary closure, Management asked you to take the night shift for a change. Letting them down is never an option!

Freddy, Bonnie, Chica, and Foxy are Fazbear Entertainment's biggest assets. Your duty is to protect them and the restaurant's reputation. Your contract calls it "a matter of life and death."

You've heard rumors that the animatronics get somewhat *lively* after hours, but no one's better equipped to handle them than you, twenty-two-time Employee of the Month!

As night watchman, you'll face many choices that lead to various outcomes. If you find an item that might help you do your job, write it down for later on the page provided. Now for your first big decision . . .

> ➤ IF YOU WANT TO PLAY ON *EASY* DIFFICULTY, ADD <u>PAPERCLIP</u>, <u>SCREWDRIVER</u>, AND <u>FLASHLIGHT</u> TO YOUR INVENTORY AND TURN TO PAGE 2
> ➤ IF YOU WANT TO PLAY ON *NORMAL* DIFFICULTY, START OUT WITH ONLY YOUR WITS AND TURN TO PAGE 2
> ➤ AT ANY TIME, YOU CAN TURN TO THE BACK OF THIS BOOK FOR SOME LINED PAGES IF YOU NEED TO MAKE NOTES FOR YOURSELF

Night 1—12:00 a.m.

The Security Office at Freddy Fazbear's Pizza is practically a second home, you've spent so much of your time here over your career. Probably *too much* time cooped up in a glorified closet, staring at a buzzing, flickering monitor until your eyes dry out. But everyone's gotta make a living—and you have an eleven-year-old daughter, Coppelia, to provide for.

You often feel like the only thing you're good at is protecting others, even at your own expense.

The office is always dark since there aren't any outside windows, but somehow at night it still manages to give you the creeps. You're probably just spooked because you're all alone in the restaurant, aside from Freddy, Bonnie, Chica, and Foxy. Animatronics aren't fantastic conversationalists, but boy, can they sing and dance!

Of course they've also been known to do . . . other things. Rumor is, they've become strangely aggressive lately. But surely those glitches were ironed out or they wouldn't have reopened this place. Not that customers have exactly been flocking back just yet.

After the restaurant closes and everyone is gone, the animatronics enter roaming mode and walk around to prevent their servos from locking up. You hear heavy footsteps echoing out there now. *Clomp. Clomp. Clomp.*

➤ TURN TO PAGE 3

If animatronics encounter you in the restaurant at night, they *should* ignore you, but your safest bet is to stay in the office until 6:00 a.m. when they return to the stage, enter sleep mode, and recharge. Then you can go home!

Management cares about their employees, and it's time-consuming and expensive to hire and train new ones—not to mention the occasional legal fees and the hassle of covering up "accidents"—so they installed reinforced doors on either side of the office. In the unlikely event that an animatronic visits you here, you can open and shut the east and west doors by pressing the big red buttons in the doorways. The light switches below them illuminate the East and West Halls outside your office so you can see whether anything is out there.

Surviving the night probably seems like a low bar for a job, but this isn't just about collecting a check. You may have to venture out of the office from time to time.

The animatronics are clumsy. And mindless, naturally. If they break something out there, you have to go fix it and clean up the mess right away so the restaurant is ready to open (just in case any customers show up). Think of the children!

Of course your number one concern is making sure nothing happens to Freddy, Bonnie, and Chica. Oh, and don't forget Foxy.

Do not forget about Foxy.

➤ TURN TO PAGE 4

There are three security monitors on the desk, but two of them are always on the fritz. Replacing them would let you see more, but you guess Management spent the money on those doors instead. You use the control panel in front of you to switch the one working display to feeds from various cameras around the restaurant.

You check the stage first. Your heart pounds when you see Bonnie and Chica are gone—so that's who you heard walking around the restaurant. Freddy's just hanging out up there on his own.

The brown bear is dapper as always in his black top hat and bow tie. You're glad they restored the vintage animatronic with his classic look. Freddy doesn't wander much, as if he's above all that just because he's the star of the show. Or maybe he's saving his energy for something.

I'm the star of this show, you tell yourself as you switch over to the Pirate Cove camera. Foxy is shy; the curtains are drawn, so he must still be back there.

Before you locate Bonnie and Chica, you discover a situation that demands immediate attention: The lights in the men's Restroom are out. You must replace the light bulbs before your shift ends. And it's better to do it sooner than later.

➤ IF YOU INSPECT THE DESK, TURN TO PAGE 5
➤ IF YOU EXIT THROUGH THE DOOR ON YOUR LEFT, TURN TO PAGE 6
➤ IF YOU EXIT THROUGH THE DOOR ON YOUR RIGHT, TURN TO PAGE 7
➤ IF YOU CHECK THE CAMERAS AGAIN, TURN TO PAGE 8

The new day-shift security guard left quite a mess! Scrunched up food wrappers and empty soda cups everywhere. You know it can be hard to stay awake while watching cameras for six hours, but there's an unspoken rule in this office: Keep it clean for the next person. You're going to have to leave a passive-aggressive note before you finish tonight. They'll never make Employee of the Month with an attitude like that!

Just because we don't often meet our fellow employees doesn't mean we aren't part of the same Friendly Fazbear Family™. It's important to have some pride and consideration. This is one of the reasons you agreed to record those training videos for new hires and leave phone messages as part of orientation—it helps you feel a connection to the other guards.

You hope hearing a calm voice helps them keep a level head when things get tense. And it's nice to know that even after you leave this job, part of you will always remain here.

You yank open the top metal drawer and yup, more trash. You pluck out the crumpled balls of paper and soda cups and spot something small and shiny at the bottom of the desk: a paperclip. Those always come in handy! You slip it into your pocket and finish tidying up the office.

All those soda cups remind you about the Restroom and those broken lights you have to take care of.

➤ ADD <u>PAPERCLIP</u> TO YOUR INVENTORY AND TURN BACK TO PAGE 4

Eager to fix the Restroom lights and get back to keep watch, you head out of the office through the west door. It's pretty dark in the hallway, but you have the layout memorized, even after the recent renovations. (They like to move things around here a lot, maybe to confuse the animatronics?) The Supply Closet is just ahead on your left. You want to stop there to pick up some fresh light bulbs, since the bathrooms aren't always stocked. You'd hate to have to make a second trip.

You yank the door open and try to step inside the closet, but you bump into something big. Solid. Furry.

And wearing a bloodred bow tie. Bonnie!

You recoil, raising your hands in a futile defensive gesture. An ear-splitting shriek cuts through the night as the six-foot-plus rabbit lunges from the shadows!

The last thing you see before everything goes black is his massive jaw snapping open and shut.

GAME OVER
>TO TRY AGAIN TURN TO PAGE 2

The Restrooms are located on the east side of the restaurant, so you head through the door on your right. You glance at the Rules for Safety poster as you exit the Security Office. You don't know why they're posted in this corner where kids shouldn't be, anyway. The rules certainly don't apply to you, especially number 8: "Leave before dark."

You laugh nervously.

The hallway is decorated with cheerful stars and a checkerboard stripe matching the floor tiles, but the dim light from the lone fixture overhead makes the fading decor seem almost sinister, especially the vintage character posters for Chica, Freddy, and Bonnie.

What was that?

You thought you heard something, but it was far off. A clanking sound, maybe from the Kitchen? The kind of sound a six-foot-tall animatronic chicken might make if it knocked a metal pot off a counter. You pause and strain your ears to listen, but you hear nothing more.

You reach the Dining Area. An overhead light illuminates six long tables already prepped for a party with confetti tablecloths and party hats lined up. You start to make your way to the Restrooms, but you freeze at the sound of slow, heavy footsteps.

➤ IF YOU HIDE UNDER A TABLE, TURN TO PAGE 9
➤ IF YOU HURRY TOWARD THE BATHROOM, TURN TO PAGE 10
➤ IF YOU KNOCK OVER A TABLE AS A DISTRACTION, TURN TO PAGE 11

It's always a good idea to check the monitors to see where the animatronics are at any given time, especially if you're thinking about leaving the office. You quickly click through the camera feed. Freddy is on the stage, but he's moved since the last time you looked in on him. He's facing the camera now, his eyes seemingly gazing into your soul as if to say, "I know that you're watching."

You shudder. *Who watches the watcher?*

White eyes peer from behind the curtain in Pirate Cove and then blink out. *Not so fast, Foxy!*

You can't find Chica anywhere, but the camera in the Kitchen has been broken for a while. It only picks up audio, no video. Something is in there, rattling pots and pans and banging cabinet doors. The giant yellow chicken has a voracious appetite. Sounds like she's a bit peckish and looking for a midnight snack.

Bonnie . . . Where's Bonnie? There!

In the West Hall, heading toward the Security Office.

➤ TURN BACK TO PAGE 4

You scramble under a table and lie on your stomach, peering out from under the tablecloth. Now you feel the vibration of footsteps as well as hear them. They plod toward the Dining Area. The animatronic would be moving faster if it knew your location.

If you make a break for it and stay low behind the tables, you might be able to reach the Restrooms without being spotted. Or you can cower here silently and hope whoever it is moves on soon.

➤ IF YOU KEEP WAITING, TURN TO PAGE 12
➤ IF YOU HURRY TOWARD THE BATHROOM, TURN TO PAGE 10
➤ IF YOU HAVE THE BONUS ITEM, YOU MAY USE IT ON PAGE 46

You don't like being out in the open here. If you can make it to the Restroom, you can try to block the door to keep the animatronics out while you replace the light bulbs.

You race toward the Restroom, the rubber soles of your shoes squeaking on the red-and-blue vinyl tiles. But remember, the animatronics are surprisingly fast when they want to be.

You only make it halfway across the Dining Area before powerful yellow arms grab you from behind. Your bloodcurdling scream drowns out the whir of animatronic servos and cracking bones.

GAME OVER
>TO TRY AGAIN TURN TO PAGE 2

A loud noise might distract the animatronic long enough for you to slip by. Tipping over a table will make another mess for you to clean up later, but the important thing is to make sure there *is* a later.

You grab one side of the table and heave, flipping it. It falls with a crash, knocking over a row of plastic chairs and sending shiny paper hats flying. That should do it.

You're about to dart toward the Restrooms when you spot both Bonnie and Chica in your way. They see you at the same time and dash toward you.

You spin around and run away—right into Freddy Fazbear's crushing embrace.

GAME OVER
>TO TRY AGAIN TURN TO PAGE 2

They say discretion is the better part of valor, so you keep hiding and waiting. Definitely not because you're too scared to budge.

The footsteps cease, and you wonder if the animatronic is waiting for *you*. You clamp a hand over your mouth and count the dried, pale wads of gum stuck to the bottom of the table.

Seven. Gross!

After several minutes, which seem more like an hour, you're pretty sure the coast is clear. From your vantage point on the floor, you don't see any oversize animal feet in your immediate vicinity.

It's time to make your move.

➤ IF YOU HEAD STRAIGHT TO THE RESTROOM, TURN TO PAGE 13
➤ IF YOU CHECK THE TABLETOP FIRST, TURN TO PAGE 14

You step into the men's Restroom and shut the door. The antiseptic scent of bleach still pervades the air, which is far from the worst thing you've whiffed in there.

You try to look around, but it's too dark with both lights out. That's why you're here!

What are the odds that two bulbs would burn out at the same time? Maybe there was some kind of power surge; after all, the wiring in the building is ancient. That's probably why the cameras always glitch and monitors in the Security Office keep overloading.

That might even explain some of the strange behavior exhibited by the animatronics. Unless . . .

You shake your head. You're in the dark when it comes to that stuff. In this case, literally. *Just focus on your job,* you think. *Focus on getting home to Coppelia.* Everything else is way above your pay grade.

➤ IF YOU REPLACE THE FIRST LIGHT BULB, TURN TO PAGE 15
➤ IF YOU LISTEN AT THE DOOR, TURN TO PAGE 16
➤ IF YOU INSPECT THE SINK, TURN TO PAGE 17

You crawl out from under the table and grab it to pull yourself up. Your legs are a bit shaky.

There isn't a lot on the table. The flimsy white vinyl tablecloth is decorated with colorful confetti. It's disposable so after a party the staff can just scoop up all the plates, food scraps, and other detritus and toss it all into a garbage bag. It's wasteful, but faster and cheaper than having to launder dozens of fabric tablecloths post–children's birthday parties every single day.

Five pointed party hats with different-colored stripes are lined up in the middle of the table. Something shiny catches your eye: a foil **Gum Wrapper**.

You sigh and slip it into a pocket to discard later. People just leave their trash wherever they feel like it. This wouldn't have happened in the old days, when working at Freddy Fazbear's Pizza was a badge of honor. The franchise has truly fallen on hard times, thanks to those pernicious rumors about missing kids—and the lingering bad press from "the Bite of '87."

If only the victim could tell what he did to provoke that attack, but he doesn't talk anymore. Or do much else. So the press completely blew the incident out of proportion, and the place hasn't been the same since. That makes it a little easier for you to be moving on.

But you're going to be a model employee right up to the end.

➤ ADD GUM WRAPPER TO YOUR INVENTORY AND TURN TO PAGE 13

How many night watchmen does it take to change a light bulb?

None. They refuse to do it, because if they chase away the night, they're out of a job.

You smile to yourself as you take a detour to retrieve a step stool and new bulb from the maintenance closet. You often make up jokes in your head while you're working, and you can't wait to get home to inflict your latest creations on Coppelia.

She'll groan loudly and say affectionately, "Bad joke, Dad."

You'll remind her that telling dad jokes is a mandatory requirement of all fathers. And you never shirk on your duty.

The boring, real answer to the question is, of course, "one." You finish twisting the new bulb inside the socket and say, "Let there be light" as it flickers on, casting the bathroom in its warm glow.

You blink as your eyes adjust from the darkness. The white porcelain urinals and sinks are gleaming. This is the cleanest the bathroom will be all day. Once the restaurant opens and kids are unleashed to eat and play, this will quickly become one of the most disgusting rooms in the facility.

One light down, one to go.

➤ IF YOU REPLACE THE SECOND LIGHT BULB, TURN TO PAGE 18
➤ IF YOU LISTEN AT THE DOOR AGAIN, TURN TO PAGE 19
➤ IF YOU INSPECT THE SINK, TURN TO PAGE 20

Maybe the darkness is making you paranoid, but you press your ear against the door and listen. If an animatronic follows you into the Restroom, it won't be great for you. There's only one way out.

At least I'm in the best place for a person to lose control of their bladder. You chuckle and wince as the sound echoes around you.

The restaurant sounds quiet, which oddly makes you feel even more nervous. The darkness seems to be pressing in on you, making it hard to breathe, even harder to think. Your imagination is running wild without any sensory inputs.

All you want to do is replace the light bulbs and get back to the Security Office as quickly and safely as possible.

➤ IF YOU REPLACE THE FIRST LIGHT BULB, TURN TO PAGE 15
➤ IF YOU INSPECT THE SINK, TURN TO PAGE 17

Plink. Plink. Plink.

That dripping faucet is so annoying, you can't concentrate on anything else. You turn to your right and feel for the sinks as you edge along the wall. When you reach them, you tighten the hot and cold water taps until the drip stops.

The sink is filled with water. It appears that something is clogging the drain. You probe it and feel something soft and slimy. You pry it loose and squish it in your fingers. It's slightly sticky. You raise it to your nose and sniff tentatively.

Chewed gum. Ew!

With the obstruction removed, the water drains out of the sink, gurgling down the pipes.

➤ ADD <u>CHEWED GUM</u> TO YOUR INVENTORY AND TURN BACK TO PAGE 13

You've just removed the second burned-out bulb when you hear something big run up to the Restroom door.

Foxy, you think just before he busts the door open. The tattered crimson fox gapes at you, one eye covered with a black patch, jaw hanging slack to reveal vicious teeth. His right arm is raised threateningly with a sharp silver hook on the end where his hand should be.

Everything about this animatronic screams "Not for kids," which is probably why his attraction has been marked OUT OF ORDER for the reopening. Though as far as you know, he's never bitten any *kids*.

But now Foxy is literally screaming and rushing toward you. You hurl the light bulb in your hand at him, but it shatters harmlessly against his head and broken shards of glass tinkle on the floor tiles. Great move—now he's *really* agitated.

The good news is, you won't have to clean up the mess. The bad news is, *you* are the mess.

GAME OVER
>TO TRY AGAIN TURN TO PAGE 2

Your caution pays off. You hear footsteps outside, moving much more quickly than Bonnie or Chica usually do. Getting louder by the second.

While you've been in the Restroom, you haven't been keeping an eye on Pirate Cove! Foxy must have left his attraction. You hope he didn't hear you working in here, but he does have big ears—they're among the few parts that still function on the tattered old animatronic.

Yeah. He's on his way to the Restroom right now, and you don't have much time before he gets to you.

➤ IF YOU BARRICADE THE DOOR, TURN TO PAGE 21
➤ IF YOU HIDE IN A STALL, TURN TO PAGE 22

One of the sinks is lower than the other to make it easier for kids to reach the faucets, just as one of the urinals is at a child's height. It's a thoughtful detail in a place designed for children and families.

Heavy feet are running in the Dining Area. The sound rapidly gets louder. You barely have time to process what's happening when the door bursts open. You see glowing white eyes and in the dim light recognize the tall, lean silhouette of Foxy the Pirate. His wicked sharp teeth and the metal hook on the end of his right arm glint in the dark bathroom.

Seeing Foxy up close usually sends a thrill through you. You used to stop in to see him every day at the end of your shift, until they closed his attraction and warned everyone to stay out of Pirate Cove.

The tattered animatronic rushes toward you in an eye blink. Your combined screams reverberate deafeningly in the bathroom.

Your final thought before the darkness becomes permanent is, *But you were my favorite!*

GAME OVER
>TO TRY AGAIN TURN TO PAGE 2

You can't lock the door because kids always find a way to get themselves trapped inside the Restroom, so you look around for something to shove against it. The trash can doesn't look heavy enough—and you're out of time. Foxy is outside!

The door moves inward and you lean your back against it, pushing it closed again with all your might. As if your life depends on it—which it does.

The light bulb you just changed starts flickering as Foxy's metal hook bangs and scrapes against the door. Each impact sends a jolt through your body, vibrating in your bones. You hope Foxy will just go away, but he just keeps pounding on the door and screeching. Sweat pours down your face and your feet slide on the slick tiles. You're losing your grip, on the bathroom door and on reality.

The door opens enough to let him get his metal hook inside. The pointed tip is an inch away from your right eye.

All you have to do is hold the door until 6:00 a.m. . . .

Unfortunately you can't even hold it for six seconds.

GAME OVER
>TO TRY AGAIN TURN TO PAGE 2

Hide! You have to hide!

You can't fit in the maintenance closet. It's too small and crammed full of mops, buckets, and cleaning supplies. Your only option is to duck into one of the stalls and stand on the toilet, like you did in elementary school when you needed to get away from the mean kids.

Now that you think about it, maybe that's one of the reasons you became a security guard, so you could help those who can't help themselves. Of course you imagined that you would be armed in order to protect and serve, but weapons of any kind aren't allowed at Freddy Fazbear's Pizza. Nothing kills a kid's party more than seeing someone with a taser hanging out in the corner, even if he is the good guy.

You dash to the first bathroom stall but find that it's locked from the inside! It's secured with a simple slide bolt latch. You might be able to get it open if you had something thin enough to fit between the door and jamb.

➤ IF YOU BARRICADE THE RESTROOM DOOR, TURN TO PAGE 21
➤ IF YOU TRY THE NEXT STALL OVER, TURN TO PAGE 23
➤ IF YOU HAVE A <u>PAPERCLIP</u> AND WANT TO USE IT, TURN TO PAGE 24

The next stall over is open, but before you can get inside it, the bathroom door bangs open and slams against the wall, loud as a gunshot.

Foxy the Pirate is here, and he knows how to make an entrance.

His exposed metal feet clink against the floor as he steps into the bathroom. The porcelain tiles crack under the pressure of his weight. His eyepatch is pulled up so both of his glowing white eyes are focused intently on you.

He scrapes his hook along the wall as he stalks toward you. And then he starts humming.

Foxy used to sing in stage shows with Freddy, Bonnie, and Chica, until he was banished to Pirate Cove and left to be forgotten. The tune is slow and unsettling, but you can't quite remember the song, at least not in the short time you have left.

GAME OVER
>TO TRY AGAIN TURN TO PAGE 2

You check your pockets for the paperclip you found earlier. Got it!

You straighten out the wire and then bend one end of it up in a right angle. Foxy isn't the only one with a hook now! You insert your new makeshift tool between the door and frame and fiddle around.

It only takes you a second to catch the knob of the bolt and slide the lock open. The door swings out toward you. You slip into the stall and pull the door closed.

You don't believe this: The door won't stay shut! The slide bolt is jammed now—oops!—and you can't lock the door. What rotten luck.

Foxy's footsteps stop right outside the Restroom. What now?

➤ IF YOU TRY THE NEXT STALL OVER, TURN TO PAGE 23
➤ IF YOU HOLD THE DOOR SHUT, TURN TO PAGE 25
➤ IF YOU HAVE <u>CHEWED GUM</u> AND WANT TO USE IT, TURN TO PAGE 26

You try to hold the stall door closed, but it's difficult to maintain a grip on the small knob of the broken slide bolt latch. It keeps slipping from between your finger and thumb.

The Restroom door bangs open loudly enough to make you wince. The crash echoes along with heavy, clanging steps on the tiled floor.

It's definitely Foxy. His plush costume is worn away and tattered all over, leaving his endoskeleton legs and feet completely exposed.

Why is he still here? He should have left the Restroom when he didn't find anyone inside. *Please go away, Foxy.*

The stall door rattles in its frame as you shift your precarious hold on it. It's an almost imperceptible sound and movement, but you hear the servos of Foxy's ears as they swivel in your direction.

My, what large ears you have. You suppress a mad giggle as panic overcomes you.

A horrible scream rends the air, and the stall door is yanked out of your grasp as Foxy rips it right off its hinges. He rushes toward you, eyes wild and mouth wide.

GAME OVER
>TO TRY AGAIN TURN TO PAGE 2

You pull the wad of chewed gum from your pocket and pick lint off it. It's still soft and slightly sticky. You wedge it into the door lock and the door stays closed.

You sigh with relief and crouch on the toilet, tucking your feet under you and out of view. The Restroom door creaks open and bumps against the wall. Someone is there, waiting in the doorway.

Waiting.

Watching.

Waiting.

Somehow you manage to remain perfectly still and eventually whoever it is leaves.

➤ IF YOU OPEN THE DOOR AND LOOK OUTSIDE, TURN TO PAGE 27

➤ IF YOU PEEK UNDER THE STALL, TURN TO PAGE 28

You quietly open the stall door and tiptoe to the door. The heavy footsteps are growing more distant. You take a quick look outside the Restroom and see Foxy ambling through the Dining Area on his way back to Pirate Cove.

You wipe a sleeve across your damp brow. *Whew!* That was close. Your fingers ache and twitch from holding the stall door closed. You are going to file a very stern complaint letter to the maintenance staff for leaving a stall door broken until the next shift.

You check your watch. It's just after 4:00 a.m., and you still have a job to do.

➤ TURN TO PAGE 29

You lower yourself gently to the floor of the stall, freezing any time you make the slightest sound and waiting for a moment before you continue. Soon you are lying on your belly, grateful that the Restroom has been so thoroughly cleaned.

You peer out from under the door. No sign of the metal legs and feet of Foxy's exposed endoskeleton. From here, you can glimpse a sliver of the Restroom hallway and beyond that, the Dining Area.

All is quiet.

You lie there for a few more minutes to be sure you're alone and to settle down and catch your breath. That was too close!

You're getting nervous about being outside the Security Office, with its cameras and door locks to make you feel, well, more secure. But before you can head back there, you need to finish your job for the night.

➤ TURN TO PAGE 29

You stare up at the second broken light bulb.

"You're the only thing standing between me and home tonight," you say.

"So, I'm talking to inanimate objects now. And myself. That's awesome."

You've been through a lot already. You're tempted to leave now, knowing that someone on the day shift will have to replace the bulb (and fix that bathroom door) if you don't. But like you said in one of your training videos for the restaurant, "You can't spell *team* without M and E."

After the Bite of '87, you heard some of the staff twist that around to "You can't spell *teàm* without M-E-A-T." You didn't much appreciate that. People deal with tragedy and loss in their own ways, sometimes with humor. But hey, at least it shows that they were listening during orientation!

➤ IF YOU REPLACE THE SECOND LIGHT BULB, TURN TO PAGE 30
➤ IF YOU LOOK INSIDE THE SECOND BATHROOM STALL, TURN TO PAGE 31

You replace the second light bulb even faster than the first.

The later it gets, the more dangerous it is to be outside the Security Office. You haven't been watching the cameras, but you have to assume all the animatronics are walking around now.

With the bathroom once again bright and cheerful, you can head back to safety. But getting there will be very unsafe.

You return the step stool to the maintenance closet and dispose of the old burned-out bulbs in the trash. You glimpse your reflection in the wide mirror. You look . . . terrible. The light reveals deep shadows under your eyes.

Transitioning from the day shift to the night shift is already starting to fatigue you, making you question what's real and what isn't. At least it's only for a week, and then you can rest as much as you want before diving back into your job search.

A position is opening up for a security guard at your daughter's school, and you really hope you get it! But middle schoolers can be just as difficult to handle as animatronics. In some ways, Freddy, Bonnie, Chica, and Foxy are just big, terrifying kids.

You hope you don't run into any of them on your way back to the office. Better hurry—your shift is almost over.

➤ IF YOU LEAVE THE RESTROOM RIGHT AWAY, TURN TO PAGE 32
➤ IF YOU LISTEN AT THE DOOR, TURN TO PAGE 33

The close call with Foxy has you on edge, jumping at shadows and constantly glancing over your shoulder. You're pretty sure the second bathroom stall is empty—so why do you hear hoarse, garbled whispers coming from inside?

You can't make out the words, but it sounds like someone is reciting poetry or a song or . . . a children's rhyme? Or maybe it's a jingle from a TV commercial. Something something "stains" . . . Something something "remains"? It's probably an ad for laundry detergent. But where's it coming from?

You pull the door toward you slowly.

Empty.

Or not quite. A ballpoint pen is lying on the floor at the base of the toilet. You don't know how the cleaning crew missed that, but you're definitely going to shove it in their face. You step into the stall and retrieve the pen. The door of the stall bumps closed behind you.

Your pulse quickens as you imagine yourself being trapped in here, but you force yourself to turn around calmly. That's when you see the words written on the inside of the door in angry scribbles of ink:

IT'S ME.

Weird. You'll have to leave a note for the crew to scrub that off first thing in the morning. And you'll be sure to suggest to Management that they add "No vandalism" to the list of rules.

You exit the stall and go to replace the second broken light bulb.

➤ ADD BALLPOINT PEN TO YOUR INVENTORY AND TURN TO PAGE 30

You can't wait to return to the Security Office, so you yank open the bathroom door—

Bonnie is in the doorway!

The six-foot-tall rabbit animatronic looks down at you with malevolent red eyes, groaning softly. His strained voice sounds uncannily human.

You only have a split second to act, if it isn't already too late.

➤ IF YOU SLAM THE DOOR, TURN TO PAGE 34
➤ IF YOU TRY TO SLIP PAST HIM, TURN TO PAGE 35

You're itching to get moving, but you press your ear to the bathroom door and listen. It sounds quiet out there.

You grab the handle and are about to open the door when you glance down. Faint light from the Dining Area seeps in from under the door, but it's interrupted by two shadows.

Those could be feet, you think. *Really big feet.*

The moment stretches out for a long time. Your knuckles are white, you're gripping the door handle so tightly. But then the shadows are gone and you hear footsteps moving away. You've been breathing shallowly this whole time, worried you'd be heard, so you take in a deep breath.

It's now or never!

➤ TURN TO PAGE 36

You slam the door in Bonnie's grinning face and hold it shut.

He doesn't try to get in. He continues groaning for a short while and then you hear his footsteps moving away.

Phew. That was too close a call. There's no telling what Bonnie wanted with you. You just hope he's on his way back to the stage and won't be waiting for you at the Security Office.

➤ TURN TO PAGE 36

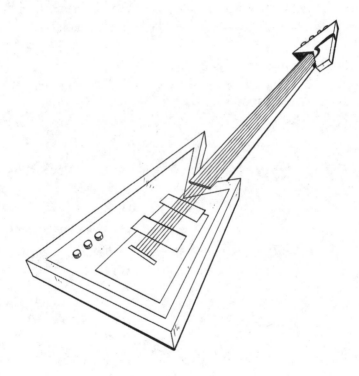

Bonnie seems bulky and slow. You think you can slip past him and run away.

You're wrong.

As you exit the bathroom, he seizes your left arm in a viselike grip. No matter how much you pull and push, you can't get free. The more you struggle, the more he squeezes your arm. The pain is excruciating as your bones break.

He ignores your screaming and drags you roughly across the Dining Area by your broken, useless arm. You go limp, dragging your heels to try to slow him down, but he carries you as easily as his electric guitar.

Your throat is raw; you can't scream anymore, and there's no one to hear you, anyway. The agony causes you to drift in and out of consciousness. You're vaguely aware that Bonnie has taken you Backstage, where animatronic parts are stored for eventual maintenance.

He drops you on the floor and turns to pick up a spare yellow Freddy costume. He walks toward you with it while you use your good arm to scoot away from him.

Bonnie wants to put you inside the suit for some reason, even though there's no way you can fit inside along with all its motors and servos.

If you manage to live through the experience, you'd be surprised at how much of you he manages to squeeze in.

GAME OVER
>TO TRY AGAIN TURN TO PAGE 2

You sneak back to the Security Office without encountering any more animatronics. By the time you get there, it's 5:45 a.m. Your shift is almost over!

You check the cameras. To your relief, Bonnie, Chica, and Freddy are all present on the stage, and the curtain is drawn at Pirate Cove.

Previous night watchmen have reported the animatronics behaving strangely, but like everyone else, you dismissed their wild stories. Sometimes people fall asleep staring at the camera feeds and they imagine things, bolstered by the old rumors and stories. The mind can be a funny thing, making it hard to distinguish hallucinations from reality.

Now you feel bad for not believing them. And you know that if you tell others about what happened tonight, they won't believe you, either. Perhaps they would even discourage you from talking about what you've seen.

You would never do anything that would harm Freddy Fazbear's Pizza. You've put too much time in, put so much of yourself into your job that you're practically a part of it yourself. You never pictured yourself leaving, but it seems like the best time to go, especially considering everything that happened tonight.

Just four more shifts left. You can do this.

➤ IF YOU TIDY UP BEFORE THE END OF YOUR SHIFT, TURN TO PAGE 37

➤ IF YOU SIT DOWN AND WAIT FOR 6:00 A.M., TURN TO PAGE 38

➤ IF YOU HAVE THE BONUS ITEM, YOU MAY USE IT ON PAGE 45

You start putting the Security Office back together the way it should be for the next shift. You toss all the garbage from the desk into the trash can. The sight of those food wrappers and soda cups sets your stomach growling—you haven't eaten in the last six hours.

You clear out junk from the yellow lockers at the back of the room as well, including a year-old packet of toaster pastries that you choke down anyway because you're that hungry. *Yum.*

You return to the desk. Five minutes to go. You click through the cameras; the animatronics are still where they belong. Already the events of the night are starting to seem like just a bad dream.

Your attention falls on the poster behind the TV. CELEBRATE! it implores in bright bubble letters above a group photo of Bonnie, Freddy, and Chica. These lovable characters couldn't be capable of the horrors you've just experienced, could they? Maybe you've just been misinterpreting everything. This place can have that effect on people when it's late, and you're tired and hungry. And lonely.

You stare at the image while moving your head from side to side. From some angles, it looks like there's a bulge in the paper. Before you can investigate, a red light starts blinking on the telephone.

> ➤ IF YOU INVESTIGATE THE POSTER, TURN TO PAGE 38
> ➤ IF YOU CHECK THE PHONE, TURN TO PAGE 39
> ➤ IF YOU WAIT FOR THE END OF YOUR SHIFT, TURN TO PAGE 40

You lean over the desk to get a closer look at the poster. There's definitely a bump on the wall under Freddy Fazbear's nose, giving it a 3D effect.

There's one thing you've always wanted to do to Freddy, but the pizza place has rules, and you're a stickler for rules. You even wrote some of them.

Number 6: Don't touch Freddy.

You poke your index finger at Freddy's nose and are surprised to hear a *honk*! Even more surprising: something behind the poster falls to the floor with a soft clatter.

You push the chair out of the way and crawl under the desk; it's even more disgusting down here, with crumbs and something dark and sticky on the dingy old carpet.

It's just soda, you tell yourself, wiping the palm of your hand vigorously on your pants.

Way at the back, you find a thin plastic card lying next to the wall. You haven't seen one of these in a long time. They stopped issuing them to employees because there was so much turnaround. This is one of the old security badges, but the face and name have been scratched out.

Whose was this? And who hid it here?

➤ ADD <u>ID CARD</u> TO YOUR INVENTORY AND TURN TO PAGE 40

The black office phone is dusty but the handset is smudged. There are smaller smudges on the 1 and 9 buttons. Someone has used it recently.

Some people around here know you as "The Phone Guy" because of your voice messages that are forwarded to new hires with reminders, tips, and encouraging words to support them during their orientation week.

Ironically, you don't use the phone much yourself. You record the messages, and Management schedules them to go out automatically. They've probably been using the same ones for ages. Maybe you should update them before you go.

A faded scrap of paper taped to the phone has a handwritten list of extensions of various locations around the pizza place: Backstage, Parts and Service, Dining Area, Party Room 1, Pirate Cove. Another number is provided for Voicemail.

The red light continues blinking on the front of the phone. Someone has left *you* a message.

➤ IF YOU CALL BACKSTAGE, DIAL THE EXTENSION ON PAGE 41
➤ IF YOU CALL HOME, DIAL THE NUMBER ON PAGE 42
➤ IF YOU CALL VOICEMAIL, DIAL THE NUMBER ON PAGE 43

You watch the clock on the desk as the numbers flip over from 5:59 to 6:00 a.m.

Yay! You survived your first night at Freddy's.

All is quiet as you leave the Security Office and pass through the restaurant. You step outside and take in the fresh, cool air, happy—and grateful—to be alive. Even the early morning light seems too bright after the darkness of the pizza place. You lose all sense of time in there, since most of the windows are in different parts of the restaurant.

There isn't a cloud in the sky. It looks like it's going to be a beautiful day. Too bad you'll have to sleep through most of it once you send Coppelia off to school. And then it won't be long before you're back here for your second night. Who knows what that will bring?

You lock up the restaurant, wave good-bye to the sleeping animatronics inside, and head home.

➤ TURN TO PAGE 229

You pick up the handset and dial the extension for Backstage. The line rings. And rings. And rings.

The line crackles and clicks intermittently, but no one picks up. You're not sure what else you expected. You're here alone tonight with the animatronics, and it's not like they can answer the phone.

And they certainly can't pick up the phone and call *you*.

Still, as you replace the handset, you feel an odd sense of relief. This has been such a strange night, part of you wondered (worried?) whether someone would pick up.

At this point, nothing at Freddy Fazbear's Pizza would shock or surprise you. But that comes from having worked here for so long. You've seen almost everything . . . right? That's why you're somewhat happy to be working the night shift: new experiences!

You hope when you're done, you can help put those rampant rumors about the animatronics to rest and make sure the next person in this chair knows exactly how to survive in this job for a long time. It's the perfect way to close this chapter of your life.

➤ TURN TO PAGE 40

You'll be home in less than an hour, but you really want to hear your daughter's voice right now, to make sure she's okay. And to let her know that you're okay. A parent never stops worrying.

You pick up the receiver and dial your home phone number, but all you hear are a series of clicks and silence. No ringing, no dial tone.

Then you remember: You have to dial a code to access an outside line. But you can't remember anyone ever telling you what it was. You bet Management doesn't want anyone calling outside the pizza place when they're supposed to be working, especially during a security shift.

It seems like a bad policy, though. What if there was an emergency, and you had to call the police or fire department? At least you won't have to deal with Management's eccentricities for much longer.

As you replace the receiver on the phone, a nagging thought in the back of your mind wonders if you made a mistake keying in your home phone number. You shake your head. This first night has been so unsettling, your imagination is really running wild. You're sure you have nothing to worry about.

➤ TURN TO PAGE 40

That blinking red light captures your attention. You don't remember whether it was there when you returned to the office or whether it appeared while you were tidying up. You assume it's an automated message sent by the system, but you can't quell your curiosity about it.

You pick up the receiver and push the flashing red button, which automatically dials Voicemail.

"Welcome to the Freddy Fazbear's Pizza Answering Service. Please enter your four-digit access code at the sound of the beep. *Beep.*"

> IF YOU HAVE THE FOUR-DIGIT VOICEMAIL CODE, TURN TO PAGE 44
> IF YOU DON'T HAVE THE CODE, HANG UP AND TURN TO PAGE 40

You enter the code and are prompted to press 1 to listen to a new message. You do so, and the message begins playing. It takes you a moment to realize you're listening to your own voice.

"Hello! Welcome to your first security shift. I'm taping this message to help you get settled on your first night and prepare you for your new and exciting career path.

"First, here's a greeting from Management: 'Welcome to Freddy Fazbear's Pizza: a magical place for kids and grown-ups alike, where fantasy and fun come to life. Fazbear Entertainment is not responsible for damage to your property or person. Upon discovery of damage or if death has occurred, a missing person's report will be filed within ninety days or as soon as property and premises have been thoroughly—'"

You hang up. You know the rest. It's strange to listen to a recording of yourself, especially one from so long ago. If you remember correctly, your daughter had just been born—a big reason why you couldn't take the night shift yourself at the time. One of your employee perks is family discounts, but for some reason you've never brought Coppelia here. Not even on Bring Your Child to Work Day.

Especially not then.

You sounded so young. So naive. You wish you could talk to that guy and give *him* some tips instead of the reverse.

Strange that the system sent an old recording. Must be a glitch.

➤ TURN TO PAGE 40

You're looking forward to retiring from this place, but you also just realized that this is the beginning of the end for you. You only have so many nights left at Freddy's, and that's kind of bittersweet.

You're feeling a bit nostalgic and thinking about your legacy as "The Phone Guy," so you decide to leave a message for the next person in this chair. Only this time, you want to tell them the truth, everything they need to know to make it here.

Well, not *everything*. Management screens these messages, so you'll have to insert some strong hints.

You don't remember the number for the Voicemail system on the office phone, but this mobile phone has it on speed dial. You connect to the messaging service.

Beep.

"Hello? Hello, hello? Uh, I wanted to record a message for you . . . to help you get settled in on your first night. Um, I actually worked in that office before you. I'm . . . finishing up my last week now, as a matter of fact, so . . . I know it can be a bit overwhelming, but I'm here to tell you: There's nothing to worry about . . ."

You run through the introductory greeting they always make you read and then touch on some important details, like how the animatronics will be on the move, and how to engage with them (or rather, *not* engage with them). That endoskeleton stuff.

All the things they should really tell you when you sign up.

➤ TURN TO PAGE 40

You wait for the animatronic to leave, but it doesn't seem to be in any hurry—it's just pacing back and forth. Even though it hardly matters which one it is, you want to know anyway. You scoot forward excruciatingly slowly, half an inch at a time, until you can see its feet.

Its giant rabbit feet.

I thought a rabbit's foot was supposed to be lucky, you think. Bonnie could be here all night. If he heads back to the stage to recharge just before 6:00 a.m., you won't have enough time to fix the light bulbs in the bathroom before your shift ends.

And then it's good-bye, Employee of the Month streak.

This is your last week on the job, but you've put so many good years of your life into it, you'd hate to throw it all away and ruin a perfect record.

Suddenly, you remember the mobile phone you have. Maybe you can use that somehow. If you call another phone in the restaurant, it might distract Bonnie. Or, you could call for help. The animatronics aren't supposed to behave like this, and you worry they will only get worse if you don't do something.

➤ IF YOU CALL THE SECURITY OFFICE, TURN TO PAGE 47
➤ IF YOU CALL ONE OF THE PARTY ROOMS, TURN TO PAGE 48
➤ IF YOU CALL BACKSTAGE, TURN TO PAGE 49
➤ IF YOU CALL THE POLICE, TURN TO PAGE 50

You pull up the contact list and click on SECURITY OFFICE. You hear the line ringing, but the office must be too far away for Bonnie to hear it.

But Bonnie hears something. He freezes at the other end of the room. You imagine his ears twitching and swiveling around. Then he starts moving. Fast.

In *your* direction!

He hears the line ringing from the receiver of your mobile phone. You end the call, but he's already on his way and he'll reach your hiding spot in seconds. You might be able to distract him if you call somewhere close quickly!

➤ IF YOU CALL ONE OF THE PARTY ROOMS, TURN TO PAGE 48
➤ IF YOU CALL BACKSTAGE, TURN TO PAGE 49
➤ IF YOU CALL THE POLICE, TURN TO PAGE 50

You pull up the contact list and click on Party Room 2. The line rings in the mobile phone's receiver, and then a second later, you hear a ringing phone from the far end of the Dining Area.

Bonnie freezes right in front of the table you're hiding under. You think he's somehow found you, but he turns and is gone. His footsteps recede as he heads for the party rooms north of your location.

You grip the phone tightly as it continues to ring, trying to keep your hand from shaking. Your plan worked! But it won't take Bonnie long to realize no one is in the party room, and then he'll come looking again. Better not waste this opportunity.

➤ PROCEED TO THE RESTROOM ON PAGE 13

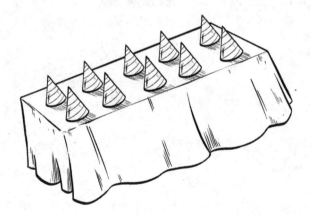

You pull up the contact list and click on Backstage. You can barely hear the phone ringing in the distance, but it's loud enough to get Bonnie's attention. He runs off toward the sound of it.

You keep it ringing on your mobile phone and climb out from under the table, so you can get to the Restroom before Bonnie returns or another animatronic comes after you. As you stand, the line clicks.

Someone picked up the Backstage phone!

You squeeze the mobile phone in your hand and listen, holding your breath so as not to make a sound.

Garbled whispering . . . the sound of a child crying. And then a deep, distorted voice in a burst of static says, "It's me."

➤ IF YOU RESPOND WITH, "WHO ARE YOU?" TURN TO PAGE 51
➤ IF YOU HANG UP AND PROCEED TO THE RESTROOM, TURN TO PAGE 13

There's no number for local law enforcement in the phone, so you just dial 9-1-1. The line rings twice before a woman answers.

"Hello, this is 9-1-1. I'm Wendy. How can I help you?"

The animatronic's footsteps are coming closer, so you don't answer.

"Hello? Anyone there?" Wendy says.

"Yes," you whisper back.

"I didn't catch that," Wendy says.

Bonnie walks away again.

"Yes," you say.

"Are you in trouble? Say yes or no."

"Yes." You swallow.

"Where are you located?"

"Freddy Fazbear's Pizza," you say.

"Freddy's? I thought they closed up. After that horri—" She draws in a shaky breath. "I didn't take those calls, thankfully, but I heard the recordings and, well, it wasn't pretty."

"Freddy's is open, except, uh, for right now because it's the middle of the night, of course. So yes, um, we're closed, but just for the night."

"Kids like to pull pranks, trying to break in there after dark. No good will come of it. You wouldn't catch me there at night. You'd have to be a grade A idiot to—"

"I'm the night watchman, Ralph," you say.

She's quiet for so long, you think you may have been disconnected. "The night watchman? Then what are you calling me for?"

"There's something bad here. The animatronics, um, they—"

Something snatches the phone from your hand and ends the call. You scream as you're dragged out from under the table.

GAME OVER
>TO TRY AGAIN TURN TO PAGE 2

"Who are you?"

Static crackles in the receiver, and then the line goes dead.

The phone is dead, too, shorted out or the battery drained or . . . something. The screen is dark and the keys no longer respond. It feels surprisingly cold in your sweaty hand.

You shake your head. You hear a child laughing, even though the call was disconnected. But there can't be a child here, not at this hour.

You call out, "Hello? Who's there?"

The laughter continues, increasing in volume. You can't stand the grating sound of it anymore. You drop the mobile phone and clamp your hands over your ears.

The sound doesn't lessen at all. It's in your head. It's in you.

You start laughing along with it, even when something grabs your legs and pulls you backward, out from under the table. You keep laughing as you are dragged across the Dining Area and toward Backstage, where an empty animatronic suit awaits you to complete it.

GAME OVER
>TO TRY AGAIN TURN TO PAGE 2

Night 2—12:00 a.m.

You yawn. "Time to make the donuts." You usually start your shifts repeating the well-known catchphrase from those donut commercials, but there aren't any coworkers here to laugh along with you.

Eh, the only people who ever laughed were the new hires—the first time you said it, and they were only being polite since they thought you were their boss. But you're nothing if not consistent. It was easy to do the right thing every day at work here, but at night . . . It's hard to know what the right thing to do is. You're in unfamiliar territory.

Fortunately, you're not only consistent, you're persistent. You never give up trying until you get the job done. You hope that's one of the better qualities Coppelia picks up from you.

You also hope you'll be around for a long time to teach your daughter even more lessons about how to live and survive in the world as she grows up. As much as you love this job, you want more for her future than a dead-end career as a security guard.

Most importantly, you hope that if anything happens to you on the job, she stays far away from Freddy Fazbear's Pizza.

➤ IF YOU CHECK THE SHOW STAGE CAMERA, TURN TO PAGE 53
➤ IF YOU CHECK THE DINING AREA CAMERA, TURN TO PAGE 54
➤ IF YOU CHECK THE RESTROOMS' CAMERA, TURN TO PAGE 55

You punch the button for the Show Stage. Freddy and Chica are both there as they should be, but Bonnie has already left.

No, wait! Bonnie is still there—most of him, anyway. His body is on the stage, but his head is gone.

Who would steal the head of an animatronic bunny?

Punk kids, you think. Daredevil teens from the high school and community college sometimes try to break into the restaurant. If they succeeded, they would want to bring back a souvenir of their "bravery."

You laugh, imagining someone shouting, "Bring me the head of Bonnie the Rabbit!"

Of course if anyone actually succeeded in breaking into Freddy Fazbear's Pizza after hours, they would be the ones in danger of losing their heads. Figuratively and literally.

But this is no laughing matter. You have a real problem now: You have to find and reattach Bonnie's head before the place opens in the morning. As terrifying as animatronics can be to some young children, they'll really freak out if they're greeted by a headless one.

Or maybe no one would notice?

➤ CHECK THE DINING AREA CAMERA ON PAGE 54
➤ CHECK THE RESTROOMS' CAMERA ON PAGE 55
➤ CHECK THE BACKSTAGE CAMERA ON PAGE 56

You punch the button for the Dining Area. Just like last night, the tables are set for a big party, with tablecloths and party hats all laid out. You wonder if the room was used at all—it looks exactly the way it did yesterday, as if nothing has been touched. Or the staff is simply meticulous about placing everything exactly where it should be. When you do the same job day in and day out for years, you get pretty good at it.

There *is* one thing out of the ordinary: Bonnie's head lies in one of the aisles between the party tables. It must have fallen off and rolled down there. It's a good thing that happened after hours because nothing sets off customers more than a malfunctioning animatronic. A head detaching and bouncing off the stage would probably result in some kids needing therapy, not to mention their parents.

Are Bonnie's eyes looking at you? The head is lying on its side, but his eyes are trained right on the security camera. Is it a warning? A cry for help?

You shake your head. It's just an optical illusion. And indeed, when you look back at the monitor, Bonnie's eyes are looking in a different direction.

You need to go reattach Bonnie's head and make sure this doesn't happen again, especially during a performance.

➤ TO EXIT THROUGH THE RIGHT DOOR, TURN TO PAGE 59
➤ TO EXIT THROUGH THE LEFT DOOR, TURN TO PAGE 60

You punch the button for the Restrooms. The camera pans back and forth, and you're glad to see everything appears normal. Normal for Freddy's, that is.

The light bulbs you installed yesterday are still going strong. You feel good that countless patrons were able to relieve themselves during the day, thanks to your efforts.

Better news: There aren't any signs of wandering animatronics outside the Restrooms. Maybe you're in for a quiet night. It sure would be nice to finish out the week with your sanity intact.

➤ IF YOU CHECK THE DINING AREA CAMERA, TURN TO PAGE 54
➤ IF YOU CHECK THE PARTY ROOM'S CAMERA, TURN TO PAGE 57

Maybe Maintenance had to remove Bonnie's head to work on it, and no one told you. (No one ever tells you anything.) If so, the head would probably be in the Parts and Service area behind the stage.

You switch over to the Backstage camera. A large metal endoskeleton rests at the end of the worktable. You see masks for Chica and several variations of Freddy, but no Bonnie head. Power cables dangle down from the ceiling.

That's a fire hazard if I ever saw one, you think. You consider raising your concern with Management, but they hardly ever take employee suggestions. A little voice inside you says it might not be a bad thing if this place burned down.

As long as it doesn't happen until after you collect your last paycheck. And no one—human, at least—is in the building at the time.

You also notice an empty Freddy Fazbear costume propped up in the corner. At least you assume it's empty. You're curious, but not curious enough to go back there and check.

The camera pans across the room once more, and you notice there are no parts for Foxy the Pirate back there.

Foxy!

You quickly switch over to the Pirate Cove camera. The curtain is wide open and the cove is empty.

Too late. Footsteps run toward the office.

Foxy bursts inside and screams in your face.

GAME OVER

➤ TO START FROM THE BEGINNING, TURN TO PAGE 2
➤ TO TRY THIS NIGHT AGAIN, TURN TO PAGE 52

You don't usually bother checking the camera outside Party Rooms 1 and 2 because it's always cutting out, but you want to be thorough, and there's a chance it will show something, so you punch the button.

Sure enough, the camera is borked. The picture is staticky and pixelated, with no audio. Fortunately, as far as you can tell, there isn't much to see. The doors to both rooms are open and everything seems to be in order: no messes, no wandering animatronics. Just like in the Dining Area, tables are set for a party that may or may not ever happen, the way things have been going.

These party rooms haven't even been used in a while. They're only needed when there are too many parties booked for the Dining Area— everyone wants to be in view of the animatronic stars on the Show Stage on their special day.

That reminds you: Coppelia's birthday is coming up next month. Whatever you will be doing to celebrate, it will not involve Freddy Fazbear's Pizza. You might even take her on a trip out of town. It would be nice to get away from all this for a while.

➤ IF YOU CHECK THE DINING AREA CAMERA, TURN TO PAGE 54
➤ IF YOU CHECK THE PIRATE COVE CAMERA, TURN TO PAGE 58

You punch the button for Pirate Cove. The shimmery, star-spangled curtains around the attraction are drawn, but you could have sworn you saw something moving back there just as the monitor switched over to the feed. The sign out in front reads SORRY! OUT OF ORDER.

You made that sign and placed it there yourself, the day they decided to shut Pirate Cove down and sealed Foxy inside. What a terrible day.

You crave order, you *need* order in your life—that's what called you to security. You keep order, like sheriffs in the Wild West. Only instead of a star-shaped badge, yours is a shield decorated with Freddy's face, proudly identifying you as security for Fazbear Entertainment. It's one of your most prized possessions. And you're going to have to turn it over in four days.

That OUT OF ORDER sign has plagued you for too long. It's a reminder that things around here have very much not been in order for a long while now. It's just taken you some time to see it, and to admit to yourself that there's nothing you can do to change it.

Since nothing is moving at the Show Stage or Pirate Cove now, this is the best time to head out . . . to find Bonnie's head.

➤ GO TO THE DINING AREA ON PAGE 59

You arrive at the Dining Area. Bonnie's head is lying on the floor, staring vacantly at the stars and streamers hanging from the ceiling. But something else catches your attention: The doors to Party Rooms 1 and 2 are closed.

Those were previously open when you saw them on camera, but the feed in that section is notoriously glitchy. It's possible you didn't see them clearly the first time.

You're the night watchman, so you should check out anything suspicious, and this is *definitely* suspicious. Those party rooms are a perfect hiding place, and it's not like the animatronics to go around opening and closing doors.

You still have to take care of Bonnie, but it's not like his head is going anywhere.

So much for an uneventful night.

➤ IF YOU GO GET <u>BONNIE'S HEAD</u>, TURN TO PAGE 61
➤ IF YOU CHECK OUT PARTY ROOM 1, TURN TO PAGE 78

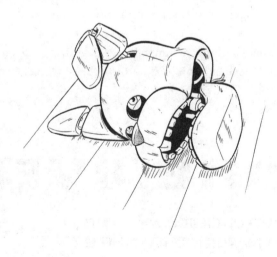

You step out into the West Hall and once again remember you've been meaning to clear out the broken TVs piled up outside the office. Those things are supposed to work for decades, but they keep burning out. It must be the old electrical wiring in this place. Wires are literally hanging down the wall in front of you, but you're pretty sure they aren't live.

You don't touch them, just in case.

As you turn down the hallway and glimpse the poster of Freddy Fazbear on the wall, you pause for a moment. You've seen it hundreds of times, but you could have sworn it just changed to show the animatronic ripping off his own head. Terrifying.

When you turn back, it's just the same old poster: Freddy singing into his microphone with LET'S PARTY! over his head. It must have been a trick of the flickering light at the end of the hall, and you've still clearly got Bonnie's head on your mind.

As you hurry toward the Dining Area, the light blinks off. Your eyes adjust to the darkness, and you see a shadow waiting at the far end of the corridor. *Just an afterimage*, you think, continuing. Then the light comes back on and Foxy is standing there, and unfortunately he is very real.

With no one checking on him in Pirate Cove, he's come out to play.

You spin around and run back to the Security Office. Foxy's footsteps sprint behind you.

In this life-and-death race, Foxy is faster.

GAME OVER

➤ TO START FROM THE BEGINNING, TURN TO PAGE 2
➤ TO TRY THIS NIGHT AGAIN, TURN TO PAGE 52

Bonnie's head is what you came here for. You walk over and pick it up. Oof! It's heavier than it looks, and something sticky leaks onto your hands. Machine oil, hopefully? You're glad it didn't leave a mess on the floor.

Even after all this time, this is the closest you've been to an animatronic. One reason being the smell—these things haven't been washed in . . . ever? There's something sharp and sour about the stench, like food left out to rot, or roadkill. You wrinkle your nose. It's very unpleasant.

You've also never touched an animatronic before—which of course is strongly discouraged! The fur is matted and kind of greasy. There are probably things crawling inside it. You don't want to hold this any longer than you have to. You turn it around in your hands until Bonnie is looking at you.

"Let's get you patched up," you say.

Bonnie's eyes blink and swivel toward you. You're so startled, you almost drop the head. It probably just happened because you were moving it around.

You look up at the stage. Bonnie's torso is still up there, and so is Freddy Fazbear. But now Chica is gone.

Should you go up and try to reattach the head, or look for tools and instructions at Parts and Service behind the stage?

➤ IF YOU GO UP ONSTAGE, TURN TO PAGE 62
➤ IF YOU GO BACKSTAGE TO PARTS AND SERVICE, TURN TO PAGE 65

You climb up onto the Show Stage and look out, imagining an audience of boisterous kids and frazzled parents. Staff and customers are not allowed up here. The last time a kid found his way onstage during a performance . . . You shudder.

That's what liability waivers are for.

Where Chica usually stands, you see a metal plate. The animatronics recharge on those at night, through battery terminals on their feet.

You gently place Bonnie's head back on his body. The animatronics deserve your respect. When you think about it, you wouldn't have a job without them. They have some flaws, but they've brought so much happiness to families over the years. That fact needs to be weighed against their actions. None of us are perfect. We all make mistakes, right?

Bonnie's head wobbles. You can't leave him like this. It seems you can tighten it by turning it, but which way: left or right?

Does it matter? You probably can't make him any worse. But maybe you should pop Backstage and see if there are some instructions. You're just a Security Officer; you aren't trained in repairing the animatronics, and if you do this incorrectly, you could lose your job earlier than planned.

Or worse.

➤ IF YOU SCREW THE HEAD ON TO THE LEFT, TURN TO PAGE 63
➤ IF YOU SCREW THE HEAD ON TO THE RIGHT, TURN TO PAGE 64
➤ IF YOU GO BACKSTAGE, TURN TO PAGE 65
➤ IF YOU HAVE THE BONUS ITEM, YOU MAY USE IT ON PAGE 66

You twist Bonnie's head to the left and something clicks inside. His eyes focus on you.

Is he fixed?

His head starts twitching and his mouth opens wide. You glimpse another set of teeth deep inside his maw. *Are those human teeth?*

He is clearly not fixed.

You step back, or try to, but his right hand holds on to your jacket. You tug at it, but there's no breaking his grip.

"No!" you cry. "I'm trying to help you!"

You manage to slip out of your jacket and stumble backward, but you fall and the back of your head slams against the stage floor. Bright lights flash in your eyes and you black out.

When you come to a moment later, Bonnie is holding your head between his oversize hands. He stares at you with unblinking red eyes, mouth jittering open and closed.

"Please don't," you whisper. "I have a daughter."

He turns your head hard to the left with a sickening crunch.

GAME OVER

➤ TO START FROM THE BEGINNING, TURN TO PAGE 2
➤ TO TRY THIS NIGHT AGAIN, TURN TO PAGE 52

You twist Bonnie's head to the right and something clicks inside. His eyelids blink once as the head comes back online. It seems you've done the trick, but there are three small holes around the base of his neck to secure the head.

This is probably why Bonnie's head fell off in the first place. As he dances and strums his signature red bass guitar on the stage, the screws vibrated and eventually fell out. And then, off with his head!

You look around the stage and find two silver screws, but no matter how much you search, you can't find the third one. Two will have to do for now. The best you can do is let Maintenance know and they can hunt down another screw tomorrow.

You insert one screw in each side of his neck. With them sticking out like that, Bonnie reminds you of Frankenstein's monster. That's no good. You'll have to tighten them or his head will tumble off again. "A job half-assed will never last," as your father used to say.

He was a perfectionist, and nothing you did was ever good enough. You vowed you would never treat your own child that way, and so far you haven't with Coppelia.

The sooner you fix Bonnie, the sooner you can go back to the Security Office, and the better your chances of getting home to her in the morning.

➤ IF YOU TIGHTEN THE SCREWS WITH YOUR FINGERS, GO TO PAGE 67
➤ IF YOU HAVE A SCREWDRIVER, USE IT ON PAGE 68

You open the door at the back of the stage marked Employees Only. Though you're an employee, you've never needed to go back here before.

You step into the Backstage area, what staff has taken to referring to as P&S, Parts and Service. It's dark and practically shouts, "This area is off-limits!" It feels wrong and a little dangerous to be back here.

You look around for something useful to help you reattach Bonnie's head properly. A user manual would be nice. An endoskeleton sits on the end of the workbench next to a screwdriver, perhaps intended for the empty Freddy Fazbear suit tucked into a corner. Another empty Freddy head rests on the other end of the workbench.

There are several Freddy heads here. They're old designs—some of them don't have eyebrows or have a slightly different shape. There is also a Chica head on the shelf, and next to it is a flashlight.

What about Foxy? You don't see any of his parts back here.

As if you summoned him, you hear heavy footsteps running toward the room! You have to find something to defend yourself with or take your chances and hide.

➤ IF YOU GRAB THE SCREWDRIVER, TURN TO PAGE 70
➤ IF YOU GRAB THE FLASHLIGHT, TURN TO PAGE 71
➤ IF YOU PUT ON THE FREDDY HEAD, TURN TO PAGE 72

You may not know how to fix Bonnie, but you know someone who does. You pull out the mobile phone you found and scroll through the contacts. Fortunately, it has the home number for your buddy Dave in Maintenance. It's good to have friends in Maintenance, even if they always beat you at bowling and never pay for dinner.

"Who's this? Do you know what time it is?" Dave growls. "It's four a.m."

You can always count on Dave to answer his own questions. He can be a know-it-all, but he actually does know it all, so you overlook his personality flaws, especially when you need his help.

"It's four already?" you say. "Gee, time flies when you're having fun, heh."

"That you, Ralph? You losing it, calling me at this hour?"

"Getting there. Listen, I have a question. Um, a *hypothetical* question. Let's say an animatronic's head falls off. Which way do you twist it back on to reattach it?"

"You know the old saying: 'Lefty loosey, righty tighty.'"

"Great! Thanks. Sorry to bother—"

"Hang on," he says. "Which animatronic is it? Hypothetically speaking."

"Bonnie."

"Bonnie . . . Let's see. Make sure you put the center screw in first and tighten it good."

Where would said screws be? As luck would have it, you find three screws scattered across the stage.

"I don't have a screwdriver," you say.

"I'm sure Mr. Employee of the Month can figure it out." *Click.*

➤ IF YOU HAVE THE BALLPOINT PEN, TURN TO PAGE 73
➤ TO SEARCH THE DINING AREA, TURN TO PAGE 74

You tighten the screws with your fingers as much as you can and head back to the Security Office. You worry that you could have done more, but you did the best you could with the tools at hand, which were none.

The next day, you're woken up by a phone call. It's your boss.

"Ralph, today we had our biggest crowd in a long time," she says. "A reporter was even there to see how we've been doing since we reopened, and we were on track for a big comeback story. Guess what happened?"

You swallow. "Was anyone, um, bitten?"

"Worse," she says. "Turn on the news."

You switch on the small black-and-white television on your kitchen counter and twist the dial until you see a breaking news story. A sobbing child covered in cake and something that looks like blood is being interviewed, and the text scroll at the bottom reads "Some Bunny's in Trouble!"

It cuts to a video recording of the animatronic show at Freddy's. The footage shows Bonnie's head toppling off in the middle of a sick guitar riff, bouncing off the stage, and landing on some poor kid's cake. Children scream and stampede while Bonnie's eyes roll wildly.

You look away from the horrific scene. "That's awful."

"We checked the camera footage. We know you sabotaged the animatronics. Ralph, you're fired. Fazbear Entertainment's lawyers will be in touch."

GAME OVER

➤ TO START FROM THE BEGINNING, TURN TO PAGE 2
➤ TO TRY THIS NIGHT AGAIN, TURN TO PAGE 52

The screwdriver makes quick work of tightening Bonnie's loose screws. The head feels as sturdy as it has ever been. Maybe you missed a calling in repair work. The only thing you enjoy as much as keeping order and protecting people is fixing things.

After your last day here, you can start looking into other positions. It might be nice to do something that lets you work with your hands more. It would be fun to make toys. Nothing that moves like the animatronics at Freddy's—just simple toys for simple joys.

Now that Bonnie is functional again, you feel oddly exposed up on the stage, especially with Chica out there somewhere. You also have to assume Foxy is out and about right now. It's a good idea to go back to the Security Office and hope nothing else breaks tonight.

➤ RETURN TO THE SECURITY OFFICE ON PAGE 69

You return to the Security Office and slump into your seat. This job is finally getting to you, but you won't—can't—let it get the best of you. You just need a moment to catch your breath. You close your eyes and breathe in. Breathe out. Breathe in . . .

A sound startles you awake. Oh no! You've fallen asleep on the job.

After all the times you've warned night watchmen to always stay vigilant and faithfully reported those who shirked their responsibility and dozed through a shift. You're embarrassed and annoyed at yourself. It's just that you're having trouble adjusting to the later hours, and dealing with the animatronics is wearing you out . . .

You can beat yourself up later. Something woke you—a sound. Or wait. Was it *two* sounds? You're still disoriented from your unintentional nap, but you think you heard footsteps approaching the door on the left *and* someone groaning from the door on the right.

You could have dreamed them up, or you could be in imminent danger. You only have time to act on one potential threat. Your clock reads 5:55 a.m., so you only have to survive the next five minutes.

➤ IF YOU CLOSE THE LEFT DOOR, TURN TO PAGE 75
➤ IF YOU CLOSE THE RIGHT DOOR, TURN TO PAGE 76
➤ IF YOU HAVE THE <u>BONUS ITEM</u>, YOU MAY USE IT ON PAGE 77

You launch yourself toward the workbench and grab the screwdriver, knocking over the endoskeleton and making a terrible racket. You turn and hold out the tool like a dagger as Foxy bursts into the room.

He hesitates in the doorway and looks around, seeming to pay you no attention. Is he wondering why they don't have any spare parts for him? Why don't they just fix him instead of leaving him in Pirate Cove to rot behind a closed curtain?

The animatronics were all built with a purpose: to entertain children. How would you feel if you were prevented from doing what you were made for? To be trapped in the dark, listening to children living and laughing just on the other side of your curtain.

Your whole world would be that sliver of light from between the curtains, only able to see and not partake in that small slice of freedom and happiness.

While Foxy is preoccupied, you try to sneak past him, but before you can reach the door, his head snaps in your direction. He rushes at you.

You jam the screwdriver in Foxy's good eye, but it turns out the eyepatch is just for show. He lifts it up and winks at you. Then he plucks the screwdriver out and turns it on you.

GAME OVER

> TO START FROM THE BEGINNING, TURN TO PAGE 2
> TO TRY THIS NIGHT AGAIN, TURN TO PAGE 52

You dash toward the shelves and pick up the flashlight just as Foxy bursts into the room. You whirl around and press the button on the flashlight.

Luckily, the batteries inside still work. A bright beam cuts across the dark room and shines on Foxy's face.

You thought maybe you would blind him temporarily so you can slip by, but the light seems to mess him up. He freezes in place, servos clicking in confusion. You hope you won't get in trouble for breaking Foxy.

You don't know how long he'll be like this, so you decide to get a move on. You need to reattach Bonnie's head and get back to the Security Office. It will only become more dangerous to be out as the night progresses, especially once Foxy reboots.

➤ ADD <u>FLASHLIGHT</u> AND <u>SCREWDRIVER</u> TO YOUR INVENTORY AND RETURN TO THE SHOW STAGE ON PAGE 62

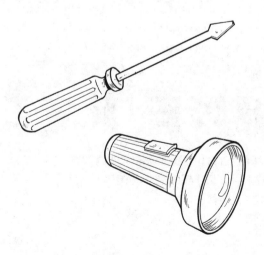

In a moment of panic, you grab the spare Freddy Fazbear mask and drop it over your own head and then stand still.

Ugh. If you thought the animatronics smelled bad on the outside, the inside of this one absolutely reeks. It smells like stale sweat, notes of old coffee, hints of cigarette smoke. Even worse, it feels warm and moist, like being inside someone's mouth. You can taste something. You don't know what it is, but it's bitter and coppery and it makes your heart flutter with anxiety.

Fear. You're tasting fear.

As soon as you put the Freddy head on, you want to tear it off again. But you don't dare, because through its eyeholes you spot Foxy standing in the doorway.

He stalks toward you and stops, only inches from your Freddy face. He leans forward to look into its eyes.

He sees you!

He screams and you black out.

You drift in and out of consciousness, distantly aware that you're being stuffed inside an animatronic suit. You hope someone checks the suits back here once in a while and finds your body, so your daughter will know why you never came home.

GAME OVER

➤ TO START FROM THE BEGINNING, TURN TO PAGE 2
➤ TO TRY THIS NIGHT AGAIN, TURN TO PAGE 52

Dave seems a little bitter about the fact that you've gotten Employee of the Month five more times than he has. But who's keeping score? All that matters is doing the best job possible, and if you receive a little recognition once in a while, that makes you feel pretty good. Plus, you guys are friends, aren't you?

Hold on. Employees of the Month get to choose a gift from the catalog, and one of those is a Freddy Fazbear's Pizza ballpoint pen *with a hidden screwdriver.*

You take out the ballpoint pen and twist the bottom off, revealing the small flathead screwdriver inside. It's too small for the screws, and they're the wrong kind, but it's better than using your fingers. You twist Bonnie's head to the right and replace the screws, making certain to start with the one in the middle.

You wonder what would happen if you inserted them in the wrong order. Or maybe Dave was just screwing with *you* and the order doesn't matter. Better safe than sorry.

Bonnie's now right as rain, but you hear footsteps out there. That must be Chica, since the last time you checked on Foxy, he was Backstage. Knowing how late it is, you decide to hurry back to the Security Office.

➤ RETURN TO THE SECURITY OFFICE ON PAGE 69

You swiftly search the Dining Area for anything useful. Under one of the tables, in a pile of cake crumbs and dirt that the cleaning crew missed, you discover a gold coin with Foxy's face on it.

It's only plastic and painted gold, of course, one of the treasure coins from Pirate Cove. It has to have been under there for some time—the Cove has been off-limits since the pizza place reopened.

The coin is just thin enough to be used as a makeshift screwdriver. You slap Bonnie's head on and twist it to the right like Dave said. From Backstage, you hear Foxy singing. And banging sounds are coming from the Kitchen. You should get out of here fast.

You use the coin to tighten the screws in Bonnie's head and call the job done.

➤ ADD THE <u>COIN</u> TO YOUR INVENTORY AND RETURN TO THE SECURITY OFFICE ON PAGE 69

You leap from your chair and close the left door. The footsteps keep approaching, but the animatronic won't be able to get in. You flip on the hall light and see the distinctive shape of rabbit ears pass by the office window.

"After everything I did for you, Bonnie?" you say.

Then you remember the other sound you might have heard. You turn and are relieved that no one is standing at the left door.

Someone groans. Right. Into. Your. Ear.

Chica jumps at you from your right and screams in your face.

You stumble away and fall against the desk. How? She must have snuck in from the East Hall while you were closing the door on the left.

You shove the office chair between you and the enraged animatronic. It's futile, but you aren't going down without a fight.

Your chest tightens. Pain shoots up and down your left arm. You clutch a hand over your heart. Your body just couldn't take one more shock tonight. Blackness creeps in along the edges of your vision. You collapse to the floor and fall onto your face.

As you gasp your last breaths, you roll over and look up. Chica looms over you.

Your final thought is, *A chicken with teeth. That's so messed up.*

GAME OVER

➤ TO START FROM THE BEGINNING, TURN TO PAGE 2
➤ TO TRY THIS NIGHT AGAIN, TURN TO PAGE 52

If someone is close enough for you to hear them groan, then they're too close. You leap for the door on your right and slap your finger against the button.

You catch a flash of yellow before the door slams shut. Looks like you were just in time.

You flick on the hall light and Chica stares in manically at you, beaked mouth wide open. You turn off the light.

"You can take your cluck and get lost," you say. "I've had enough for one night."

But it seems you haven't. The footsteps keep approaching on your left—and then Bonnie is standing there.

It's too late to close the door now. You brace yourself for the attack, but Bonnie doesn't make a move. He just stares at you.

You stare back at him. *What is he waiting for?*

You break eye contact for a moment and see the clock on the desk flip over from 5:59 to 6:00 a.m. Bonnie turns and walks away, back toward the Show Stage. At the door on the right, Chica does the same.

Did Bonnie just let you live? Was that a thank-you for restoring his head?

Or maybe you just got lucky. Either way, you survived another night and it's time to go home.

➤ TURN TO PAGE 233

You quickly grab your mobile phone and press one of the speed dial buttons. You don't know which, but you hear a phone ringing from near the Dining Area.

The groaning at the right door stops and footsteps move away down the East Hall. The steps you heard approaching the left door are gone.

Phew. Your distraction worked, and it's 5:55 a.m. You have enough time to record another message for your successor.

You call into the messaging service and start talking:

"Uhh, hello? Hello? Uh, well, if you're hearing this and you made it to day two, uh, congrats! I—I won't talk quite as long this time since Freddy and his friends tend to become more active as the week progresses. Uhh, it might be a good idea to peek at those cameras while I talk just to make sure everyone's in their proper place. You know . . ."

You keep talking and pushing buttons on the cameras until the clock rolls over to 6:00 a.m.

➤ TURN TO PAGE 233

You open the door to Party Room 1 and turn on the lights. It's basically a miniature version of the Dining Area, for private birthday parties or overflow space. When someone hosts a party here, they get a visit from Freddy, Bonnie, or Chica as part of the package, but they rarely use Freddy for such functions.

It's also company policy to have a security guard posted in each room while the animatronic is present, a duty you have often performed. But that was before the restaurant closed. Since it reopened, these rooms haven't been needed, and of course, you're on the night shift now.

Everything seems quite ordinary inside. The two long tables are covered in white tablecloths decorated with colorful confetti. Cone-shaped cardboard party hats are lined up on each table, waiting to be strapped onto rambunctious kids.

You smile, thinking back on better times. For a while, you would have said Freddy Fazbear's Pizza was the happiest place on earth, if you weren't worried about infringing on a trademark.

Approaching steps snap you back to the moment and remind you of how much this place has changed. You consider hiding, but you have plenty of time to check out Party Room 2 before the animatronic reaches you.

➤ IF YOU HIDE IN PARTY ROOM 1, TURN TO PAGE 79
➤ IF YOU OPEN PARTY ROOM 2, TURN TO PAGE 80

You're not in the mood to take any chances. You slip inside the room and behind the door and wait several minutes until the footsteps reach you.

Something stomps into the room and waits. You hold your breath, worried about making a sound. In your peripheral vision, you see a yellow blur to your left.

Chica turns off the light and the door pulls away from you, swinging closed. You wait until her footsteps recede before you open the door. Or rather, try to.

It's locked.

You're not sure how that's possible. You can only lock the door with a key because kids have a habit of pushing buttons, any buttons, and they think it's funny when they lock people out—or in. Ha ha.

Chica wouldn't have a key, but unfortunately, you don't have one, either.

You jiggle the doorknob. You pull at the door. If you keep doing that, you're going to attract more unwanted attention, and some animatronics can't be stopped by a door.

You sigh and pull up a kiddie-size chair. You strap on a party hat with silver and red stripes. You don't have any choice but to wait for your shift to end. At least you're safe while the animatronics look for you outside the room.

You'll be fired come morning, but you don't think you'll miss this job much after all.

GAME OVER

➤ TO START FROM THE BEGINNING, TURN TO PAGE 2
➤ TO TRY THIS NIGHT AGAIN, TURN TO PAGE 52

You hustle over to Party Room 2 and open the door. Or try to.

It's locked. You're not even sure who has the key to this door—these rooms aren't usually locked.

Naturally, now you're even more curious about what, or who, might be inside there.

The footsteps are closer. They're coming from the direction of the Show Stage, but you can't tell which animatronic it is. You hope you don't find out.

Unless you can figure out how to get inside this room, your only option is to try to get back to the adjacent party room and hide there instead.

➤ IF YOU HIDE INSIDE PARTY ROOM 1, TURN TO PAGE 81
➤ IF YOU HAVE AN ID CARD, YOU MAY USE IT ON PAGE 82
➤ IF YOU HAVE THE MASTER KEY, YOU MAY USE IT ON PAGE 83

You race back to Party Room 1 and close the door silently. You lean against it and listen.

The animatronic arrives two seconds later. They stop and stand outside the door for a while. You don't know how much time passes, but eventually whoever it is leaves.

You should have just taken care of Bonnie's head and forgotten about these party rooms, like everyone else has. Suddenly worried that one of the other animatronics might disturb Bonnie's head, you want to get back to the Dining Area right away. But is it safe to leave now?

➤ IF YOU OPEN THE DOOR AND PEEK OUT, TURN TO PAGE 84
➤ IF YOU WAIT A LITTLE LONGER, TURN TO PAGE 85

In movies, people use credit cards to jimmy open locked doors. You pull out the ID card you found earlier. The thin plastic is flexible but sturdy enough that you should be able to slide it between the door and the frame and push open the latch. But you'll have to be quick—the animatronic is almost here!

It actually works! The door opens and you duck inside the room and close the door behind you. The footsteps go right past and fade away.

You wipe sweat from your forehead. You switch on the lights and look around. What was so important about this room? There's no one here. It's practically a mirror image of Party Room 1, but with striped tablecloths instead of white and party hats decorated with confetti. It also has a wide window looking out at the tree line behind the restaurant and the mountains beyond that—only it's dark now, so all you see is the room reflected in the glass.

You hardly recognize yourself—or the fear in your face.

You turn your attention back to the tables. One of the party hats is slightly out of alignment with the others. You nudge it back into place, but meet some resistance. Something's under the hat!

You lift up the paper cone and find a Fazbear Entertainment branded Zippo lighter. Someone must have left it after lighting birthday candles. Tsk, tsk.

➤ ADD THE <u>LIGHTER</u> TO YOUR INVENTORY AND GO GET BONNIE'S HEAD ON PAGE 61

You open the door and hide behind it just in time. The footsteps stop in the doorway, and the animatronic makes a raspy, moaning sound as it enters the room.

It approaches the table, waits for a moment, and then leaves.

You wait until all is quiet before you step out from behind the door and resume breathing. You dare not turn on a light, but you can make out some details in the faint illumination from the Dining Area.

This is one of the few rooms at the restaurant with an outside-facing window, making it a popular choice for parties. The tables are set up just like in Party Room 1, but with striped tablecloths and party hats decorated with confetti.

One of the cardboard hats is overturned on the table closest to the door, where the animatronic stopped. You wonder why they would knock that hat over and then leave.

You close the door softly and switch on a light so you can see better. You look around and see a note pinned to the Freddy Fazbear poster marked LET'S PARTY! U READY? A message is spelled out in letters cut from a newspaper. You read it:

A Master Key is not in this game. You are the one who must live (?) with your shame. You know what they say: Cheaters don't win. But those who might try make the purple man grin.

Night 1—page 2
Night 2—page 52
Night 3—page 86
Night 4—page 121
Night 5—page 158
???—page??

➤ THE GAME HAS CRASHED

You open the party room door a crack and look out. It seems to be clear.

You open the door wider and come out. You almost step on a cupcake on the floor.

It has pink frosting and a birthday candle. It also has eyes and teeth, and it is looking right at you.

You lean down and pick it up. This is Chica's prop from the Stage Show. It's called Mr. Cupcake, though the staff has other nicknames for it.

Did Chica leave this for you? Or did it . . . somehow hop over here on its own?

You think it's harmless, but the way the eyes follow you suggests that it must be animatronic as well, though you've never seen it move before tonight.

You hold it up to your ear to make sure it isn't ticking or something. You hear the slight whirr of servos too late.

Apparently Mr. Cupcake's mouth also moves, and once his teeth bite down on something, or someone, they never let go.

GAME OVER

➤ TO START FROM THE BEGINNING, TURN TO PAGE 2
➤ TO TRY THIS NIGHT AGAIN, TURN TO PAGE 52

Though you need to get out there, you decide to wait a little longer, if only to feel safe for a few more moments. Nothing is ever what it seems at Freddy's anymore, and you can only rely on your instincts. Something tells you this is a trap. If you're wrong, you've only wasted a little time.

Your instincts were right. More than right. You look down, where faint light seeps in from the Dining Area under the door. There's a shadow there, of something small on the other side of the threshold.

You wonder what it could be. You lower yourself to the floor and try to peer under the crack. You can only see a small portion of whatever it is, but it looks like the wrapper for a large cupcake. You aren't curious enough to open the door, though. And your patience pays off.

Footsteps approach again, and you can see the distinctive chicken feet of Chica. She picks up whatever was on the floor and walks away.

That must have been Mr. Cupcake, you think. You feel silly now for being afraid of a harmless prop, but at least it's gone now and you're relatively certain that the coast is clear.

➤ GO GET BONNIE'S HEAD ON PAGE 61

Night 3—12:00 a.m.

You feel well rested and excited about going to work, just like you used to—until you step inside the dark and dreary Security Office. Somehow, all your enthusiasm deflates and you feel exhausted, as if you hadn't slept for eight hours. As if you have always been in this office, and you will always be in this office.

You settle into the seat and sigh, feeling like you've aged five years in the five seconds it took you to come in and sit down.

It must be this midnight shift. Working as night watchman, you lose touch with all the good parts of the job that motivate you each day. There are no coworkers to catch up with. You don't see the smiling kids' faces or hear their happy laughter. And you don't get to see the animatronics the way they're meant to be seen, as entertainers instead of vengeful stalkers.

When you go outside into the sunlight, your memories of the night before seem to dull and fade. When you are safe at home talking with Coppelia, you question everything that happened, and you come to the same conclusion: You imagined it. It wasn't that bad. After all, you're alive. If the animatronics were really alive and hunting you, what would be your chances of surviving one night? Two? Five?

Really darned slim.

➤ TURN TO PAGE 87

Maybe these lapses in memory are some survival mechanism. How can you go home to your daughter each morning and live a normal life knowing such horrors exist in the world? How could you leave her each night and come back to work here, knowing you might not ever see her again?

Only if you forget.

But you also have a job to do. You've always been the responsible one, even as a kid. No one had to ask you to do your homework before watching TV and riding your bike. You were, and still are, what they call an overachiever.

And yet you ended up working security at Freddy's. So many people don't understand that, but you tell them, "Some things are more important than a fancy job and a big paycheck. I love those animatronics, and I make a difference when I go to work each day."

Do you still believe that? Did you ever?

You sit up straight and switch on the security monitor. "Time to make the donuts," you mutter.

A child laughs behind you.

You spin the chair around and look behind you. There's nothing there but lockers and shadows.

Pull yourself together, Ralph. Only three more nights.

> TURN TO PAGE 88

You begin as you always do, pushing buttons. You cycle through all the camera feeds on the monitors, and everything is copacetic until you hit the party rooms.

"What the—?" You lean closer to the jittery video screen.

A table and chairs have been overturned in Party Room 2, and there is a large dark puddle on the floor. The window in the far wall is broken. A crushed paper party hat lies in the hallway outside.

"*This* is why we don't have more windows!"

Everyone always wants to schedule their parties in Party Room 2 because it has one of the few windows in the restaurant, but the moment you saw it, you knew it was a big security risk. Kids are always breaking it on a dare, though no one has ever gotten inside before.

Someone has to clean up that mess in Party Room 2.

You put your finger on your nose. "Not it," you say.

You sigh. This security job has more janitorial duties than you expected. You need supplies from the closet in the West Hall to mop the floor and board up the window.

And you should locate that intruder before they break anything else. Or get themselves hurt.

➤ IF YOU HEAD TO THE SUPPLY CLOSET, TURN TO PAGE 89

➤ IF YOU CHECK THE WEST HALL CAMERA, TURN TO PAGE 90

➤ IF YOU CHECK THE SUPPLY CLOSET CAMERA, TURN TO PAGE 91

➤ IF YOU CHECK CAMERAS FOR INTRUDERS, TURN TO PAGE 92

Still grumbling about having to clean up after other people's children, you head to the Supply Closet in the West Hall. You just want to get this over with, and it's going to take you most of the night to sweep up broken glass, mop that spill, and cover up the window. And you bet you'll be the one to get the blame for the damage, even though it happened between closing time and your shift starting.

You pull open the closet door, but you can't find the mop because there's a giant bunny in the way.

Oh crap! Bonnie!

The animatronic is suddenly in your face, head twitching violently and teeth gnashing.

The next morning, the daytime security guard is shocked to find blood spattering the West Hall right in front of the Supply Closet.

"Jeez. Some people are so lazy," he says. "The mop is *right there*."

He reaches inside the closet and starts mopping you up.

GAME OVER

➤ TO START FROM THE BEGINNING, TURN TO PAGE 2
➤ TO TRY THIS NIGHT AGAIN, TURN TO PAGE 86

You pull up the feed for the West Hall before you go out there. It shows the long corridor leading to the Dining Area, with the Supply Closet door on the left. There are several new children's drawings taped on the wall to your left, but they're unsettling images of children with fat teardrops falling from their eyes. Some of the kids have Xs for eyes.

You shudder. Kids can be so creepy. Even your daughter, Coppelia, used to draw pictures when she was younger that seemed innocent to her but felt more like threats, like when she drew you without your head for some reason, saying that it was "resting." Or the drawing of the two of you eating pancakes where she was "passing you a fork" by stabbing it into your side.

Adorable.

They're just drawings, though—they don't have to mean anything. Right?

You're about to get up and head to the Supply Closet when the light at the far end of the hall flickers and the camera goes fuzzy. They need to get an electrical engineer in here before the place gets another health code violation!

As you watch, the Supply Closet door opens. Bonnie steps out.

You cover your mouth with a hand. Bonnie walks away, toward the Dining Area.

That was a close call, but it should be safe now. For a while.

➤ HURRY TO THE SUPPLY CLOSET ON PAGE 93

You punch the button for the Supply Closet camera and nearly wet yourself when you see Bonnie waiting inside.

When you were a kid, you used to play hide-and-seek with your dad, but his tactic was to hide in places like closets and then pop out shouting "Boo!" just before you found him. No matter how much you screamed or cried or peed yourself after a jump scare, he laughed at you and kept doing it. Your dad had a mean streak. After a while, you stopped asking him to play hide-and-seek, or anything at all. Which, now that you think of it, might have been his plan all along.

When you play hide-and-seek with Coppelia, you make as much noise as possible and pretend you don't notice her peeking at you from between her fingers while she counts rapidly to twenty. You always act surprised when she finds you, in even the silliest hiding places, like under a blanket on the sofa or crouching behind the TV stand with your butt hanging out.

You never, ever hide in the closets. When *she* does, she gives you a hug after you "give up," and she comes out.

You doubt Bonnie is going to give you a hug. At least not the kind you can survive.

"Olly olly oxen free," you mutter.

Eventually, Bonnie leaves the closet. The hall camera shows him walking to the Dining Area.

➤ HURRY TO THE SUPPLY CLOSET ON PAGE 93

You cycle through each of the cameras once more, this time checking carefully for someone who shouldn't be there.

Bonnie and Chica have both left the stage.

"Why don't you go out much, Freddy?" you ask. When the camera pans away from him and back, you gasp. His head is now turned and is looking into the camera.

"You stay there." You swallow. "Please."

The curtain at Pirate Cove is open slightly, and you see Foxy grinning from the depths. "You stay there, too." If the intruder is hiding in there, Foxy wouldn't even think of leaving his new plaything.

Funny how you've started attributing thoughts and feelings to the animatronics as if they weren't simply acting according to quirks in their programming. Anthropomorphizing, you believe it's called.

You started out as a psychology major at the community college, specializing in children's psychology, before you dropped out. You figure that experience helped you get the job at Freddy's, not that you use psychology much anymore unless you're trying to convince your daughter to do something she doesn't want to.

Maybe you should have studied artificial intelligence instead.

After checking everywhere, the only place the intruder could be is in the Kitchen. There's no picture but you hear someone banging around. If someone's in there with Chica, they'd better be hiding.

➤ HURRY TO THE SUPPLY CLOSET ON PAGE 93

You open the Supply Closet in the West Hall and yelp when something reaches out of the darkness. It hits you in the face and you jerk backward.

The wooden handle of a mop falls and clatters hollowly on the black-and-white tiled floor.

You chuckle and look up at the security camera in the hall. You flash it a V sign with your fingers and then stoop to pick up the mop and return it to the bucket. Gradually, your racing pulse returns to normal.

You have two big jobs ahead of you in Party Room 2. You have to clean up that spill and broken glass and board up the window. Everything you need is right here, but you can't carry all the supplies with you. You'll have to make two trips. But you're not sure which task you should complete first.

➤ IF YOU WANT TO CLEAN UP THE SPILL AND BROKEN GLASS, TURN TO PAGE 94
➤ IF YOU WANT TO BOARD UP THE WINDOW, TURN TO PAGE 95

You hate messes, so you decide to clean that spill first. You know it will only get more difficult to wipe up if it dries. You grab a mop and the bucket, then look around for some cleaning solution.

The bottles on the shelf are all industrial-grade stuff, high concentration bleaches and stain removers. You bet this is what people use to clean up crime scenes. Despite its smell and appearances, Freddy's is a sanitary place, and Management is always reminding staff to keep it clean and tidy—at least in the public spaces.

You kick at a crumpled piece of paper someone has left in the closet and roll your eyes. But you want to set a better example, so you pick up the paper and smooth it out. It's an old newspaper clipping with an ominous headline: "Kids Vanish at Local Pizzeria—Bodies Not Found."

You hastily ball up the article again and toss it in the trash, where it belongs. *Those poor children*, you think. *Their poor parents*.

You heft a jumbo bottle of bleach. It's heavy and a lot to juggle with the mop and the bucket. Should you fill the bucket here or carry the bottle to Party Room 2 with everything else?

➤ IF YOU FILL THE <u>BUCKET</u> HERE, TURN TO PAGE 97
➤ IF YOU FILL THE <u>BUCKET</u> IN PARTY ROOM 2, TURN TO PAGE 98

Your first priority as night watchman is to keep Freddy Fazbear's Pizza secure and protect the animatronics, though you aren't sure how much protection *they* need.

You'd better make sure no one else can sneak into the restaurant in the night. You pick up a hammer and swing it around experimentally. It's no Mjölnir of Thor, but you already feel a little safer. You grab a box of nails and a pile of wooden planks that are just the right size and set off for the party rooms.

➤ ENTER PARTY ROOM 2 ON PAGE 96

What a mess! You step into Party Room 2 with dread settling in your chest. There's a wide, dark pool of liquid on the floor, and the pane from the window on the far side of the room is gone. Broken glass is everywhere. The shards on the floor twinkle in the moonlight coming through the open window. It's kind of pretty, despite the circumstances.

A cool draft from the window brings the scent of something sharp and metallic. You flip on the light and see that the puddle is red and viscous.

That's a lot of tomato sauce, you think hopefully, but when you kneel to investigate more closely, you know it's blood.

You gag and run to the window to throw up. The fresh air wafting inside settles your stomach. You've never noticed before how bad this place smells all the time, like greasy old pizza and sweat and sometimes rotting meat. And now, blood. Human blood?

"An *animal* must have gotten in," you say aloud as if that would make it true. Whatever it was, it's gone, one way or another. You just have to worry about keeping anyone else out.

You place a plank over the window and are about to hammer in the first nail when you hear strains of music from the Dining Area. It's getting louder.

➤ IF YOU TRY TO BOARD UP THE WINDOW QUICKLY, TURN TO PAGE 104
➤ IF YOU LISTEN AND WAIT, TURN TO PAGE 105
➤ IF YOU CLIMB OUT THE WINDOW, TURN TO PAGE 106

You empty the bottle of bleach, and your eyes tear up from the fumes. You pour in pine-scented cleanser, hoping it will help dilute the potent mixture and make things smell a little nicer.

You're about to lug the full bucket into the hall when you hear footsteps approach. Big, heavy steps. Bonnie could be coming back.

You shut the door and wait silently inside the closet for the footsteps to pass. Your eyes, nostrils, and throat are burning. You stifle a cough.

The footsteps proceed down the hall toward the Security Office. Good thing you aren't in there right now! You might be able to sneak out and get to the Dining Area without being noticed. You have to take the chance because you can't stay here much longer. The liquid in the bucket looks like it's smoking. Acrid fumes rise up. You blink, barely able to see anymore. It feels like ice picks are being stabbed into your pupils.

You try to open the door, but it's stuck. You push on it hard, bracing yourself against the back wall. Bottles fall from the shelves all around you and the mop tumbles. The bucket tips over and the floor is flooded with the poisonous cleaning product.

You cough and cover your mouth. Red spittle and froth speckle your palm.

"Help." You gasp. Your vision swims and then, mercifully, you pass out. In games or not, you should *never* mix household chemicals, ever.

GAME OVER

➤ TO START FROM THE BEGINNING, TURN TO PAGE 2
➤ TO TRY THIS NIGHT AGAIN, TURN TO PAGE 86

It doesn't seem wise to handle chemicals in a confined space like the Supply Closet, so you place the bottle of bleach in the bucket with the mop and drag them to Party Room 2.

You flip on the light—it's a horror show. The spill inside looks like blood. A lot of blood.

It smells like blood, too: a bitter, metallic scent you can almost taste, like copper. You gag and then throw up your dinner.

Now you have an even bigger mess to clean up. You empty the jug of bleach into the bucket and get to work, mopping up the blood and vomit. The stench and fumes might be overpowering if not for the shattered window in the far wall, which lets in fresh air.

Even though you hate bodily fluids when they're outside the body (where they shouldn't ever be), you find you enjoy work like this. When you're done, the floor is clean and no one would ever be able to tell that some person—or some animal—lost a catastrophic amount of life-giving blood in this room. If there's no evidence, it may as well have never happened. Management will be pleased.

You're so busy admiring your handiwork you don't hear the foot-steps until they're almost right outside.

➤ IF YOU HIDE UNDER A TABLE, TURN TO PAGE 99
➤ IF YOU LEAVE THROUGH THE OPEN WINDOW, TURN TO PAGE 100
➤ IF YOU HAVE THE BONUS ITEM, YOU MAY USE IT ON PAGE 101

You duck under a table and peer out from under the striped table-cloth. You recognize Chica's chicken legs, but they're splattered with red like a grisly Jackson Pollock painting. Chica walks around the room. Is she wondering what happened to the blood?

You remember the mop and bucket, next to the door. Chica knows you were here. You force yourself to lie perfectly still, breathing as shallowly as possible. Then you notice there are wet footprints leading from the bucket to your hiding spot. The floor hasn't quite dried yet.

In a flash, Chica's face appears under the tablecloth, mouth wide and screaming.

She drags you out from under the table, and you remain conscious long enough to see the floor doused in blood again and to have one final, irrational thought:

I just cleaned that.

GAME OVER

➤ TO START FROM THE BEGINNING, TURN TO PAGE 2
➤ TO TRY THIS NIGHT AGAIN, TURN TO PAGE 86

You race toward the broken window and catch Chica's reflection in a sliver of glass remaining in the frame as you dive outside. You roll in the dirt, and shards of glass slice your hands. But you clamber to your feet and run away from the restaurant.

You make it maybe thirty feet before something grabs you from behind. You tumble and see a blur of yellow fur and Chica's chicken feet. She's spattered in blood, but you aren't sure if it came from whoever broke into the restaurant or from you.

You've always told the night watchmen it isn't safe to leave in the middle of the night, it's better to wait until the end of their shift, but you didn't really know why. Just repeating what Management told you, and they supposedly have a good reason for everything. This is what happens when you break the rules.

You have only yourself to blame, but it's a shame that Coppelia will have to suffer for your incompetence. At best, you'll end up another newspaper headline. At worst, Fazbear Entertainment will cover all this up and your daughter will never know what happened to you.

If there's no evidence, it never happened.

You think Chica's going to drag you back into the restaurant, but instead she carries you into the woods. This might go even more badly than you thought—for everyone.

GAME OVER

➤ TO START FROM THE BEGINNING, TURN TO PAGE 2
➤ TO TRY THIS NIGHT AGAIN, TURN TO PAGE 86

You grab your mobile phone and speed-dial Backstage. The phone line rings on the other end of the Dining Area. The footsteps hurry off in that direction.

That bought you some time to get this mess cleaned up. With one hand pinching your nose shut, you mop quickly with the other. When you're done, you dump the bucket of bleach and pine cleanser out the broken window to lighten your load. Then it's back to the Supply Closet to get a hammer, boards, and nails to fix up the window.

You continue dialing different numbers around the restaurant to keep the animatronics moving and out of your hair, but you don't want to drain this phone battery.

You're certain the loud hammering is going to bring an animatronic or two your way, so you call the Security Office to get them as far away from you as possible. Then you board up the window and beat a hasty retreat.

In the hall outside the party rooms, you ring Backstage one more time to lure anyone away from the Security Office and clear your way back. But this time, someone picks up the phone.

The intruder? You'd almost forgotten someone else might be in the restaurant.

Static crackles on the line, and you hold your breath to listen closely. All you can hear are the faint echoes of children's laughter. Then the line goes dead.

The screen of your phone lights up with a message:

➤ RETURN TO THE SECURITY OFFICE ON PAGE 102

By the time you make it back to the Security Office, you are so done—with this night, with this job, with Fazbear Entertainment. And most of all, with the animatronics.

But it's nothing a good night's sleep can't fix. You're sure you'll be feeling much better tomorrow when you come back to work. Tonight has just been . . . a lot.

You can't stop thinking about that mess you mopped up in the party room. That pool of blood used to be a person. (Possibly. Probably not.)

Even if someone broke into the restaurant and got a closer look at the animatronics than they bargained for, no one deserves to die like that. There wasn't anything left to identify, so if anyone is waiting for them at home, they'll never know what happened. Maybe they'll be another one of those faces on the back of a milk carton.

Unless.

You didn't see any sign of the intruder in the restaurant, but perhaps they had been there all along, hiding in plain sight.

Like inside one of the unused suits in the room behind the stage?

You pull up the Backstage camera feed. Bonnie is in there now, but you're more curious about the Freddy suit on the worktable, wondering if it's actually empty. Are you curious enough to go check it?

➤ TURN TO PAGE 103

It's 5:57 a.m. Shift's almost over.

Oh well, maybe you'll get a chance to check those suits tomorrow. At the moment, you have just enough time and battery power on your mobile phone to record a message for the next night watchman—a brief one.

They'll probably never even listen to it. Most of the night-shift security guards don't stick around. You guess the stories got to them. Freddy's is spooky at night when you're alone, no doubt about that— even without animatronics roaming around who might see you as a threat.

You hope your messages help someone someday, but you're also recording them for you. They help you organize your thoughts and put some perspective on the night you just had. It's almost a sort of therapy, having a conversation with the person who will replace you, even if it's a one-sided one.

Making these messages is a way of affirming that you will be leaving and someone else will be in this chair. Just two more nights to go!

The desk clock flips over to 6:00 a.m.

➤ TURN TO PAGE 235

You love music, but hearing it in the middle of the night in an empty restaurant can't be good.

The animatronics are programmed to travel only through certain areas of the restaurant—but they're already moving beyond their approved areas and their approved actions. What if they see this open window as an opportunity to leave? In that case, you need to cover the window, not only to keep others out (for their own safety!), but also to *keep the animatronics in.*

You nail boards over the broken window as quickly as you can. Each time you hammer a nail into wood, it sounds like a gunshot.

The music is loud, too. So loud you can't even think, like it's inside your head. A killer earworm.

You can't name that tune, but you've heard it in old cartoons you watch with your daughter. It might be from some famous opera. You find yourself pounding each nail in rhythm with the music.

There! Done! You hammer the last nail just as the music stops.

Finally, I can think again, you think. And your very next thought is: *Why did the music stop?*

Broken glass crunches on the floor behind you. You turn and see Freddy Fazbear staring at you with vacant black eyes. You back up against the boarded-up window. He isn't going anywhere.

Unfortunately, neither are you.

GAME OVER

➤ TO START FROM THE BEGINNING, TURN TO PAGE 2

➤ TO TRY THIS NIGHT AGAIN, TURN TO PAGE 86

Music of unknown origin in the middle of the night feels ominous. Right now isn't the time to move or make noise.

You tiptoe to the open door of Party Room 2 and grip the handle of the hammer tightly as you listen. You've heard this song before: It's a march, played on a music box or something. As far as you're aware, none of the animatronics have a built-in music box, though you think you've seen one over by the Prize Counter.

The music comes closer and closer and closer . . . Then it moves past the party rooms and fades. You risk a peek around the open door-way and see Freddy Fazbear walking away, microphone in hand.

You choke back a gasp. This is the first time you've seen Freddy out like this, on his own. You were beginning to wonder if he'd ever step off that stage.

Now you're worried about what finally drew him out. At least he's gone, for now.

You board up the window quickly, straining to hear whether Freddy or any of the others are approaching. Now that the task is done, there's still all that blood to clean up.

So much blood.

But you've also been away from the cameras for too long. Maybe you should swing by the Security Office first to check in.

➤ IF YOU RETURN TO THE SECURITY OFFICE, TURN TO PAGE 111
➤ IF YOU GO TO THE SUPPLY CLOSET, TURN TO PAGE 107

You climb out of the broken window. A shard of glass slices your palm open, and you drip blood all the way around the restaurant to the parking lot. You get into your car and you drive home.

You're home early, so Coppelia is still sound asleep. You sit in her room, listening to her breathe, until the sun rises. Thinking. Worrying.

You abandoned your shift, and you know what that means: Don't bother coming back. Do not pass Go. Do not collect your final paycheck. You're ashamed that after a flawless career at Freddy's, it's come to this.

You're alive, but you're a coward.

As the days pass, you think you might be even worse than a coward: You're a killer, or at least indirectly responsible for the deaths of innocents.

The news reports a series of missing children over the last few nights since you escaped from Freddy's—since something else also escaped with you. Four kids have disappeared so far, and when you do a little detective work, you determine their houses are all in a line from the pizza place.

A line leading to your house.

On the fifth night outside Freddy's, you find yourself comforting Coppelia in her room while the animatronics try to get into your house, wreak havoc and revenge, and get your daughter.

GAME OVER

➤ TO START FROM THE BEGINNING, TURN TO PAGE 2
➤ TO TRY THIS NIGHT AGAIN, TURN TO PAGE 86

You make it back to the Supply Closet and then back to Party Room 2 in record time, toting a bucket, a mop, and bottles of bleach and other cleaning products.

It's disgusting work, mopping up a human body's worth of blood, but you pretend it's just food spilled on the floor.

You immediately push that thought away as it might actually be too on the nose.

You're just about done and ready to head back to the Security Office for the end of your shift. You're worn out and practically half asleep when you hear footsteps outside the door. It's nearly morning—this must be the intruder trying to escape through the window they came in!

➤ IF YOU HIDE UNDER THE TABLE TO SURPRISE THEM, TURN TO PAGE 108
➤ IF YOU CONFRONT THEM AT THE DOOR, TURN TO PAGE 110

You crawl under a party table to surprise the intruder. You wait for a long time, anticipating the expression on their face when they discover the window they broke has been boarded up and there's no way out other than the front door.

But it's you who are surprised when Freddy Fazbear stumbles into the room. You prepare to defend yourself with the mop, but there's something wrong with him. He's staggering around, bumping into tables and chairs. His suit looks saggy, and his head is on crooked.

This isn't Freddy, it's someone wearing one of the spare animatronic suits from Backstage. Now that you're looking for them, you see human eyes behind the big eye sockets of the Freddy head, a second pair of teeth in his throat when his mouth flops open.

You're about to apprehend the intruder when you notice fresh blood on the floor you just mopped: footprints, from the door to where "Freddy" leans against a table. The costume is soaked in red. Red tears seep from the eyes.

You gasp and he lurches toward you, arms dragging at his sides. He tilts his head at a strange angle to look at you under the table.

"*It's me,*" he intones. He bends over so far, the mask starts to slide off. You can almost see his real face. It's—

You wake up beneath the table. It was just a nightmare . . . ?

➤ IT SEEMS SAFE, SO GO BACK TO THE SECURITY OFFICE ON PAGE 109

You get back to the Security Office a few minutes before the end of your shift. You sit back in the chair, sipping cold coffee while cycling through the different cameras throughout the restaurant.

Maybe this job isn't so bad after all, you think. It's been a while since you checked the cameras, so it takes a moment to track down the animatronics. Freddy is hanging out in the West Hall, but it's already 5:58 a.m., so he should be returning to his charging platform soon—and you'll be going home. Chica seems to be banging around in the Kitchen, and Bonnie is in the Dining Area, on his way back to the stage.

You yawn. All in a night's work! Your eyelids are feeling heavy . . .

Suddenly, you snap them open and jolt forward on your seat. You hastily slap the button for Pirate Cove.

The curtain is wide open. The sign in front of the attraction reads IT'S ME. And Foxy is gone.

Because he's in the Security Office right now!

You forgot to keep an eye on Foxy, and now he gets to play.

But it'll all be okay, you reassure yourself, since this is all just a dream. You must still be asleep under that table in the party room. You'll wake up any minute now.

GAME OVER

➤ TO START FROM THE BEGINNING, TURN TO PAGE 2
➤ TO TRY THIS NIGHT AGAIN, TURN TO PAGE 86

You won't hide anymore, especially not from an intruder. You rush toward the door, brandishing the mop like a staff. Tonight, you're going to be the one delivering jump scares.

You swing the mop as you emerge from the room and you make contact—with Chica's head. Her left eye is knocked out. It bounces on the floor a few times and then rolls under a party table.

Oops.

Chica stops moving, sparks flying from the eye socket. She makes a sound like a whimpering child.

The next night, you find a termination notice in your locker. Management claims you vandalized Chica and even blames you for her being "covered in animal blood." You contest it, but the security footage shows you aggressively beating Chica with a mop until she breaks.

Instead of a final paycheck, you find a bill for animatronic repairs, which comes to more than you earn in a year. You beg them to cut you a break after all your years of loyal service and they finally offer you a deal: You can pay off your bill gradually as the permanent night watchman. You don't have any choice but to accept.

Now all you have to do is make it through 365 nights at Freddy's . . .

GAME OVER

➤ TO START FROM THE BEGINNING, TURN TO PAGE 2
➤ TO TRY THIS NIGHT AGAIN, TURN TO PAGE 86

Freddy went toward the Show Stage on the west end of the Dining Area, so you stick to the east side. You plan to return to the Security Office via the East Hall before continuing on to the Supply Closet to finish your tasks for the night.

But as you pass the Kitchen, you think again about the intruder who broke into the party room—and lost a lot of blood. The only place they could be hiding is in the Kitchen, since the camera is only transmitting audio. It's on your way—maybe you should duck in there to check things out.

> IF YOU STOP IN THE KITCHEN, TURN TO PAGE 112
> IF YOU CONTINUE ON TO THE SECURITY OFFICE, TURN TO PAGE 115

You slip into the Kitchen, just to make sure that no one is hiding in there. And maybe to grab a little snack, since you haven't eaten in hours. That's one of the benefits of the video feed being out in the Kitchen—no one will be the wiser. And if anyone does notice some food missing, you can always blame Chica.

You hit the jackpot! There's a yellow cupcake on the metal counter with pink frosting. An unlit candle sticks out of the center. This must have been left over from a birthday party; maybe one of the Kitchen staff meant to take it home and forgot it. You poke the frosting—it has a hard outer layer, but it's soft underneath—as fresh as food gets around here.

You lick the frosting from your finger (delicious!) without questioning the wisdom of eating random food you find lying around. You're about to pick up the cupcake when you hear footsteps approaching quickly.

You'd better get out of sight. You want to take the cupcake with you, but it might work better as a distraction if you can light the candle to draw attention to it.

➤ **IF YOU HIDE BEHIND THE COUNTER, TURN TO PAGE 113**

➤ **IF YOU HAVE A <u>LIGHTER</u> AND WANT TO USE IT, YOU MAY DO SO ON PAGE 119**

You hop over the counter and drop down behind it softly a moment before someone enters the Kitchen. Did they see you?

You crouch with your head below the counter, muscles tensed and ready to run or fight—whatever you must do to survive. A large shadow on the wall, cast by light from the doorway, suggests your visitor is one of the animatronics. The round profile looks like Chica.

The animatronic bumps into a baker's rack and a pot clatters to the floor.

Definitely Chica.

Chica has a big appetite—her bib reads LET'S EAT!, after all. But you've never seen her actually eat anything. Sometimes she carries around her little cupcake companion, or they hand her a prop pizza slice for a party.

You have a sudden image of her pecking someone to death with her beak and then using her eerily human teeth to tear into their flesh. You hold back a shudder at the horrific thought.

She's doing something at the counter, but you can't determine what. A few minutes later, she leaves the room.

You slowly raise your head to look out. Yes, Chica's gone, and unfortunately so is the cupcake you were going to eat. In its place, Chica has left her prop companion, Mr. Cupcake.

➤ IF YOU EXAMINE MR. CUPCAKE, TURN TO PAGE 114
➤ IF YOU PROCEED TO THE SECURITY OFFICE, TURN TO PAGE 115

Mr. Cupcake looks much like the birthday cupcake you just lost to Chica, only bigger with a fake lit candle and large haunting eyes. You swear those eyes follow you as you get closer to it.

An optical illusion, you think. But your hands tremble as you reach down to pick up the abandoned prop.

It's heavier than it looks, probably ten pounds easy. You assumed it would be hollow or some cheap plastic, but it's metal, and you wonder if it has some rudimentary animatronic parts inside that interact with Chica during her stage performances.

Begrudgingly, you admit to yourself that it's kind of cute.

"Guess I can't leave you in here all by yourself," you say. "Someone is liable to try to eat you!"

You can always return it to Chica later on. Maybe you can use it to distract her at a crucial moment, or it can just be a souvenir to remember your time here.

As if you could ever forget!

➤ ADD <u>MR. CUPCAKE</u> TO YOUR INVENTORY AND PROCEED TO THE SECURITY OFFICE ON PAGE 115

You make it back to the Security Office without encountering any more animatronics, but you don't get comfortable. You can't stay long, with that bloody mess in Party Room 2. But there's always time to sweep the cameras for trouble.

Freddy is missing from the stage, but Bonnie and Chica are back there already. Chica has stains around her mouth, but the black-and-white video makes it hard to identify what it is. Could be frosting from the cupcake she found in the Kitchen.

Yeah, that must be what it is.

Even Foxy is still hiding out in Pirate Cove. This night has been feeling off, and you reason it's because it's the first night Freddy has gone wandering. It's possible that the other animatronics are lying low tonight to give him some room to explore.

They're not afraid of him, are they?

You can't pick up Freddy on any of the cameras, but you do hear his music playing in the Kitchen. It's a popular spot tonight!

➤ TURN TO PAGE 116

Satisfied that you're taking only a minimal risk as long as you steer clear of Freddy's music, you stop by the Supply Closet for the second time tonight. You grab a mop, some cleaning products, and a bucket. Something rattles inside the bucket. You steel yourself for something traumatic, like a dismembered body part or a small dead animal, and look inside.

A pink water pistol is at the bottom of the bucket.

It's the kind of toy they give away at the Prize Counter if you turn in enough tickets. A cheap toy that probably won't work right and will cease working completely after playing with it just a few times. You know they buy these things in bulk for pennies a piece and then make several dollars of profit off them.

Finally, I'm armed, you think.

You raise the water gun and spin around to aim at the hall outside the closet. "Go ahead, make my night, punk."

The hall is empty. You probably scared everyone off.

You slip the water pistol into a pocket. Even though it's plastic junk, it does make you feel a little safer. Which probably says something about how *unsafe* this whole situation really is.

➤ ADD THE <u>WATER PISTOL</u> TO YOUR INVENTORY AND TURN TO PAGE 117

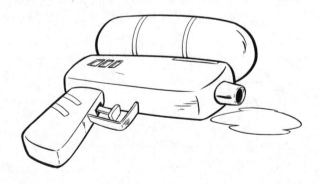

You hurry back to Party Room 2 to clean up. The puddle on the floor has dried some, so it hardly even resembles blood anymore as you apply the mop and bleach and add some pine-scented shine to the red-and-blue tiles.

To save yourself some time, you bring the cleaning supplies to the Security Office with you. The day shift can put them away, and this way everyone will know that you weren't just sitting in front of the screens tonight. You definitely put in a good night's work.

Freddy's music starts up again, and it sounds like it's right outside the office—but you can't tell which door it's coming from. It seems to be coming from all around you. You grab the desk clock—it's 5:59 a.m.—and back up, looking from one door to the other. You hear laughter and see light flash on your left.

➤ TURN TO PAGE 118

Freddy's eyes and mouth are strobing white light like a demented jack-o'-lantern while the song continues playing as if there's a music box in his head. The song is almost over, and you don't know what will happen then.

The clock flips over to 6:00 a.m. and you immediately hold it out in front of you. "It's six a.m., Freddy. Go back to your stage!" you shout. "Six a.m.!"

To your surprise, the music stops and Freddy does in fact slink off. You look at the clock in your hands, a makeshift talisman that only works once a night—at a very specific time.

The question is: Do the animatronics have internal clocks, or could you deter them by simply changing the time on this clock?

➤ TURN TO PAGE 235

You pat your pockets frantically, recalling the lighter you found earlier. There it is! You pull it out and it takes you a few tries to get a flame going; you aren't used to heavy-duty lighters like this, and it doesn't help that you're nervous.

You light the candle and then bolt around the counter to hide behind it as someone enters the Kitchen. You catch a distorted reflection of a large yellow chicken in the industrial-size chrome refrigerator door.

From that vantage point, you watch Chica approach the cupcake with interest. Something overcomes you and you begin singing "Happy birthday" softly. You're giving away your location, your only advantage, but somehow Chica keeps staring at the burning candle.

➤ TURN TO PAGE 120

When you get to the part where you name the birthday person, a name pops into your head. "Happy birthday dear . . . Susie. Happy birthday to you."

Chica lets out an anguished scream and smashes the cupcake with a hand. She storms out of the Kitchen, wailing.

Weird, you think. *Even for a walking animatronic.*

You pay your respects to the poor smashed cupcake. Chica's tantrum not only extinguished the candle's flame (did she make a wish?) but also reduced the baked good to crumbs. Which you're still tempted to eat.

Something glints in the cupcake wrapper. You poke through the mound of crumbs and find a gold ring!

It's heavy, not like the plastic, gold-painted trinkets you can get from the vending machines or the Prize Counter. How did it get here? You wonder if it belongs to the baker who made the cupcake. The ring could have slipped off a finger and into the batter.

There are no inscriptions or identifying marks: It's just a plain gold wedding band. Well, you can always check with the staff tomorrow to see if anyone is missing it. And if no one claims it, it should make a nice little parting bonus for you, or a souvenir for you or your daughter.

➤ ADD THE <u>GOLD RING</u> TO YOUR INVENTORY AND PROCEED TO THE SECURITY OFFICE ON PAGE 115

Night 4—12:00 a.m.

You know something is off as soon as you arrive for your shift tonight. Way off. It doesn't take a detective to figure that much out, because all the lights are on at Freddy Fazbear's Pizza, like it's open for business. Only it's midnight.

So maybe someone forgot to switch off the lights on their way out, but it isn't as simple as that. Like the good night watchman you are, you check the security cameras before you do anything else, and what you see has you both baffled and anxious: the animatronics are more active than usual, especially for this hour.

They seem to be having a party in the Dining Area.

Freddy is up on the stage singing his clockwork heart out while Bonnie and Chica are showing off their moves on the dance floor below. Bonnie is swinging his bass guitar around, and Chica is doing the Chicken Dance up and down the aisles, knocking chairs over. Even Foxy is joining in, so you know this is big trouble. He's dancing on the tables, crushing party hats and shredding tablecloths with his shiny metal feet.

You cover your eyes. Now, *this* is a nightmare. You don't know how you're going to clean this up, but you can't even think of janitorial duties until you shut down the party. How are you going to do that?

➤ TURN TO PAGE 122

You can't just ask them nicely to stop—they'll come right after you. With all the lights on, maybe the animatronics never switched over into Night Mode, and they don't know what to do without supervision or kids to entertain. You might be able to get them back on track if you just turn off the lights.

But you can't walk around switching off lights, either—then they'll come right after you. If only there was a way to turn off all the lights at once.

Other than praying for a well-timed blackout to make it easy for you, your best bet is to head to the Breaker Room and shut down the power to the entire restaurant. That should force their systems to reboot.

But there's a big problem: the Breaker Room is behind the stage, on the other side of the Dining Area. And sneaking through there with all the lights on without alarming Freddy, Bonnie, Chica, or Foxy would be a small miracle. If you succeed at that, you're definitely going to buy a lottery ticket in the morning.

➤ IF YOU HEAD TO THE DINING AREA AND HOPE FOR THE BEST, TURN TO PAGE 123

➤ IF YOU PACE AROUND THE OFFICE TRYING TO THINK OF ANOTHER WAY, TURN TO PAGE 124

You slip quietly down the West Hall toward the Dining Area. At the entrance to the room, you press yourself against the wall and peer inside.

Freddy and Foxy are on the stage together while a strange song plays over the speakers. You think it's a recent pop hit, but it's running backward and at a reduced speed. Every now and then you catch words and phrases in the recording that give you a chill: "death for all," "pain," "fire and knives," stuff like that.

You must be mishearing them. The human brain often tries to make sense out of nonsense, leading you to see and hear things that aren't really there.

But there's no making sense out of what Foxy is doing. His movements are jerky and erratic, less like dancing and more like . . . malfunctioning? It reminds you of watching clay models move in one of those old Ray Harryhausen stop-motion films.

Bonnie and Chica are playing games: Chica tosses party hats toward Bonnie, and Bonnie swings at them with his guitar.

You might be able to get by them unnoticed while they're preoccupied with their antics.

➤ IF YOU SNEAK ALONG THE LEFT SIDE OF THE ROOM, TURN TO PAGE 143
➤ IF YOU SNEAK ALONG THE RIGHT SIDE OF THE ROOM, TURN TO PAGE 144
➤ IF YOU SNEAK AROUND AND UNDER THE TABLES, TURN TO PAGE 145

You walk back and forth in the cramped Security Office. It may seem like a waste of energy to some people, or an annoying habit, but pacing helps you figure your way out of a bad situation. You think best on your feet, and moving around *feels* like you're doing something even if you aren't actually going anywhere.

But tonight, you feel more like a zoo animal trapped in a too-small cage. The Security Office is the only safe place at the moment, but what happens when the animatronics decide to bring the party to you? You aren't good at parties, especially costume parties where you might end up stuffed into a suit filled with robot parts.

You keep walking between the lockers at the back of the office and the desk at the front, where the TV shows the animatronics wrecking the Dining Area.

You don't know how many times you've looked at those lockers, but on your tenth or eleventh trip, you notice something new—*behind* the lockers.

A ventilation opening near the floor.

You drag the lockers away from the wall, wincing at the sound of scraping metal. Has this vent always been here? You're excited: You can use these to sneak right by the Dining Area undetected. If you can find your way.

You crawl inside and immediately face a decision:

➤ **IF YOU TURN RIGHT, TURN TO PAGE 125**
➤ **IF YOU TURN LEFT, TURN TO PAGE 127**

Picturing the floor plan of the restaurant in your mind, you anticipate that turning right will be the most direct way to the northwest corner, in the Backstage area where the Breaker Room is.

The thumps of your hands and feet as you crawl through the ventilation shaft echo around you, and the thin metal vibrates with a wobbly sound. You're surprised that the flimsy construction can hold your weight and even more surprised at how spacious it is inside—less constricting than you expected. You suppose good airflow and filtration are important in public spaces, especially where notorious disease vectors like children are involved.

These shafts are probably big enough for an animatronic to pass through, so someone your size has no trouble negotiating them.

However, it's a confusing labyrinth of passages in here. You navigate by instinct, trying to move generally toward the stage, but the layout doesn't make any sense. Some branches lead to dead ends for no discernible reason while others let out into dusty rooms you don't even recognize. It seems like whole sections of the building have been closed off over the years, or perhaps they're expansions that were abandoned before completion.

Or maybe you're just hallucinating, giving in to the darkness and the monotony and your imagination.

Whatever the reason, you're well and truly lost!

> PUSH ON AND TRY TO FIND YOUR WAY ON PAGE 126
> IF YOU HAVE THE BONUS ITEM, YOU MAY USE IT ON PAGE 137

The deeper you go, the more turned around you get. You realize too late that you should have tried to keep track of which turns you made. If only you had some string or breadcrumbs to help you find your way back to the Security Office.

You crawl and crawl and crawl until you're too tired to crawl anymore. Haven't you been in here for days? The restaurant must have opened by now, but you haven't heard any people—and they must not hear you, either.

Tired, parched, and starving, you push away your fear of animatronics and bang and shout for someone to help you. Even an animatronic tracking you would be a welcome sight right now.

At the end, you cling to the memory of your daughter. "I'm sorry, Coppelia," you croak through cracked and peeling lips.

Management knows you must have crawled into the Security Office vent, yet no one ever finds and recovers your body. At least you are never forgotten:

Occasionally, a customer will catch a whiff of you in the air, wrinkle their nose, and say, "What is that horrible smell? Did something die inside the walls?" Staff like to tell stories about the "Security Guard Who Vanished" to new employees, so they know they should never, ever crawl into a vent.

Long after you're gone, your cautionary tale saves many lives.

GAME OVER

➤ TO START FROM THE BEGINNING, TURN TO PAGE 2
➤ TO TRY THIS NIGHT AGAIN, TURN TO PAGE 121

As soon as you choose to go down the left shaft, you start second-guessing yourself. Maybe you should have turned right, to head to the northwest corner of the pizza place. You almost turn back, but you figure all these passages must lead to the same place eventually.

You don't handle confined spaces well, but these corridors are surprisingly roomy. Much bigger than they need to be. With just the endless expanses of gray metal that shift under your weight, you become sensitive to other clues about your whereabouts. One section of the vents is sticky with grease and dust, and you know you must be passing through the Kitchen. You're on the right track!

Up ahead, there's another junction, to the left and the right. Picturing the layout of the restaurant in your mind, you can't figure out what could be to the right—there shouldn't be anything there, at least no room or area you can access normally.

Turning left should point you in the direction of the Breaker Room.

➤ TURN RIGHT ON PAGE 128
➤ TURN LEFT ON PAGE 129

It gets darker as you move along the right corridor. Less light from the restaurant is seeping through the cracks and vent openings. This route must be taking you farther from the Breaker Room, but your curiosity gets the better of you.

Where are you? Are you even still in the restaurant?

Now it's basically pitch-black and even more disorienting, but you push on. Finally, you reach a dead end.

Literally. As you grope around for another path, your hand falls on something thin and dry, wrapped in threadbare fabric. It makes you think about the skeleton model in your high school biology classroom.

This is a bone, you think. You drop it with a resounding thud, but you don't examine it any further. You don't want to know if it belonged to a human. Or why it's here. You're somewhat relieved that you can't see anything, though your imagination is vivid enough to provide its own interpretation of the scene.

You turn around and make your way to the Breaker Room.

➤ TURN TO PAGE 129

You can tell you're going the right way because you hear music and crashing sounds from the Dining Area. The animatronics are going to wreck the restaurant if you don't put a stop to this and tidy up before morning.

You pick up the pace, but moving faster means making more noise because the metal shaft shakes violently under your weight. The music in the Dining Area abruptly cuts, and you freeze.

Did they hear you?

Maybe they've simply worn themselves out. If they've been operational since the pizza place closed, they haven't had a chance to recharge on the stage yet. If that's the case, all you need to do is climb out of the vent system, shut off all the lights, and somehow move the animatronics back up onto their charging platforms.

Could it really be that easy?

➤ IF YOU EXIT THROUGH THE CLOSEST VENT, TURN TO PAGE 130
➤ IF YOU KEEP MOVING FORWARD IN THE VENT, TURN TO PAGE 131

The closest vent has a grate over it, but you can see you're under the stage, facing the back curtain. There are a lot of exposed cables and levers down here, and some exposed wires you assume are live. These must power the charging platforms above your head.

It's still quiet out in the Dining Area. You start kicking at the vent cover, but it holds fast. All you manage to do is bend some of the metal grille.

You're making such a racket, you almost miss the rhythmic sound of something moving in the vents with you. You stop kicking, and at first, you think that steady thump is just an echo from your efforts, but it continues.

You peer into the darkness ahead. There's a turnoff that you assume leads to the Backstage and the Breaker Room you were heading for. Something's up there. You squint and see—

The tips of two rabbit ears.

As you're processing the fact that Bonnie is in the vent with you, he pops his head around the corner and shrieks. The horrible sound reverberates, disorienting your balance and sense of direction as you back up as quickly as you can.

But not quickly enough.

GAME OVER

➤ TO START FROM THE BEGINNING, TURN TO PAGE 2
➤ TO TRY THIS NIGHT AGAIN, TURN TO PAGE 121

You stick to the plan. Sometimes the animatronics are more dangerous when you *can't* hear them, and just because the music has stopped doesn't mean they have.

You keep moving forward. You should be hitting the Breaker Room any minute now. Your knees hurt from crawling on them, and your hands are caked with grime. You keep having to brush cobwebs and tiny spiders from your hair and neck. You are going to take a long hot shower when you get home.

You reach another corridor branching to your right, sooner than expected. Does this go to the Breaker Room or somewhere else?

➤ IF YOU LISTEN FOR CLUES TO WHERE YOU ARE, TURN TO PAGE 132
➤ IF YOU HEAD TO THE RIGHT, TURN TO PAGE 133
➤ IF YOU KEEP MOVING FORWARD, TURN TO PAGE 134

The silence makes you nervous. You don't want to move for fear of making too much noise and being detected by the animatronics. And without their music playing in the Dining Area, it's harder to orient yourself in the vents.

So you wait and listen. The only sounds you can hear are your own heartbeat pounding in your ears and your shallow breathing in the confined space.

But waiting pays off. The music in the Dining Area resumes—it seems to be coming from the corridor on the right.

The music should muffle the sound of your movement in the vent, and there's a good chance all four animatronics are still partying together in the Dining Area. You push on to get a look ahead—and there it is, the Breaker Room! Unfortunately, a grate is covering the vent, but you can see the power panel on the wall, agonizingly out of reach.

You're about to kick at the cover to try to pop it off when the music abruptly stops again. You listen, but footsteps echo in the vents from all over the restaurant. The animatronics could be anywhere and everywhere. You have to shut off the lights, and fast!

> TRY TO KICK OFF THE VENT COVER ON PAGE 135
> WAIT AND HOPE FOR MORE MUSIC ON PAGE 136
> IF YOU HAVE THE BONUS ITEM, YOU MAY USE IT ON PAGE 137

You're 75 percent sure that the Breaker Room is on your right, so you take the turn and advance slowly.

You're maybe closer to 50 percent sure you're going in the right direction, but that certainty goes down the farther you crawl. Is it possible you've gotten so turned around that you've overshot the Breaker Room and are somehow headed in the opposite direction? If you didn't know any better, you'd say you were heading toward Pirate Cove because you hear Foxy singing ahead of you.

You stop to turn around, but then you notice a dim glow ahead of you in the darkness. You head toward it, thinking it might be the exit to the Breaker Room after all. Foxy's singing gets louder—it seems to be right in front of you, but the vent has a way of bouncing sound around in disorienting ways.

Your skin raises in goose bumps, and the hairs on the back of your neck curl up. Too late, you realize that the light you're chasing is *Foxy's left eye*. He's in the vent with you!

Foxy lifts his eyepatch, and now there are two glowing eyes only ten feet away, and coming ever closer.

He makes a terrible racket as he scrabbles toward you in the metal corridor. Then he opens his mouth.

The last thing you hear is his horrible, humanlike scream reverberating around you.

GAME OVER

➤ TO START FROM THE BEGINNING, TURN TO PAGE 2
➤ TO TRY THIS NIGHT AGAIN, TURN TO PAGE 121

You decide to keep moving. If you missed the correct turn, you'll just back up and try again.

Some dust filtering down from the top of the ventilation shaft makes you sneeze. You stop and wipe your nose with the back of your hand—and it's only because you pause for that moment that you hear something moving behind you.

Thump, thump, thump, thump. Whatever it is was keeping pace with you, so you didn't notice the noise until now.

From the way the metal trembles against your palm, it's something larger and heavier than you.

Your size and speed are the only advantages you have over Freddy, Bonnie, and Chica. So you move faster, hoping you can get out of the vent before your stalker catches up.

There's the exit up ahead! And you were right—it's the Breaker Room. You put on another burst of speed.

But before you reach the end of the shaft, you feel a sharp pain in your right leg. You look back. There's a giant fishhook stuck in it. Dragging you backward.

Wait, not a fishhook—it's a *pirate* hook, belonging to Foxy the Pirate. Just your luck, as he's the one animatronic you can't outrun.

You grab on to the grate covering the vent as Foxy keeps pulling. You grit your teeth against the pain of the steel grille digging into your fingers, holding on for dear life, until you black out.

GAME OVER

➤ TO START FROM THE BEGINNING, TURN TO PAGE 2
➤ TO TRY THIS NIGHT AGAIN, TURN TO PAGE 121

You're so close to your goal, you decide to risk it and kick that cover off. If you're fast and lucky enough, you'll be able to turn off the power before anyone can get into the room.

You start kicking at the grate, but it's sturdier than you expected, considering the deteriorating state of everything else around here. Each impact of your shoe against the metal grille only seems to bend it—and make a tremendous banging noise.

"This must be why . . . they call it . . . the Breaker Room," you mutter in between kicks. "Because you have . . . to break your way in."

Someone groans.

"Fair," you say. "Not my best dad joke." Your daughter would have hated it, too. But she isn't here (thank goodness!), so who was that? You glance over your shoulder and see not a little girl, but Chica the Chicken crawling toward you, head twitching, beak snapping, eyes red.

You kick harder at the grate until it finally explodes outward and clatters against the wall, dangling by one resilient bolt. You propel yourself out of the vent and scramble to your feet in the Breaker Room. Chica screams and continues crawling toward you.

You hold up your hands and back away. "Come on, the joke wasn't *that* bad."

You're so focused on her, you're surprised when Foxy bursts through the door and gets to you first.

GAME OVER

➤ TO START FROM THE BEGINNING, TURN TO PAGE 2
➤ TO TRY THIS NIGHT AGAIN, TURN TO PAGE 121

You hold out a little longer in the hopes that the music will resume. Your patience is rewarded when a new song begins. Not the dance music from the Dining Area, but Freddy Fazbear's music box rendition of a classical piece—closer than the Dining Area and coming closer still.

You fight the urge to hide in the vent, not trusting an animatronic to sneak up behind you while you're preoccupied worrying about Freddy.

Freddy is still some distance off, so you kick at the metal vent cover until it finally pops free and clatters to the floor. The music is louder now, and the tune is almost over. You don't want to find out what will happen when it ends.

➤ CRAWL INTO THE BREAKER ROOM ON PAGE 138

Each time you shift your weight in the ventilation shaft, the metal groans and the footsteps outside pause. When they resume, they're closer. It's only a matter of time before the animatronics get into the Breaker Room, and then you won't be able to stop them.

Or worse, they may get into the vents.

A distraction would buy you some time.

You take out your mobile phone. The battery indicator is low—you've been using it intermittently for days and you don't have the right charger for it. Hopefully, it can get you through the rest of the week.

You want the animatronics as far away from you as possible, but you know if you dial the Security Office phone directly, they won't hear it and be drawn to it. So you dial a series of numbers in sequence to lure them away. First the Dining Area. You hear the phone ringing and the footsteps close by move toward it.

It's working!

You wait thirty seconds and dial Pirate Cove. You can barely hear that phone from here, the sound echoing in the vents. After another thirty seconds pass, you call the Security Office. You can't hear the phone ring from here, but you trust it has taken some of the heat off you. You keep the line open while you kick off the ventilation grate. It falls to the floor with a clatter that you hope won't bring the animatronics right back.

➤ CRAWL INTO THE BREAKER ROOM ON PAGE 138

This room is unfriendly to human life. Exposed power conduits run along the ceiling and power cables, and wires dangle down the walls and from the ceiling. You don't want to touch any of them! The air around you buzzes with electricity. It's at least twenty degrees warmer in here than anywhere else in the restaurant.

It would be really easy for a fire to start in here, you think. No one would ever question it.

Sweat drips down your forehead and back as you study the power control panel. There are five round buttons, like elevator buttons, faintly glowing green.

Green is good. That means they're on.

You should be able to just push them to turn off power to each area of the restaurant, but you don't know whether you need to press them in a certain order or risk shorting out the entire system.

All your life, you've gotten used to *not* pushing buttons, especially when you don't know what they do, but it seems like that's your official job lately.

Well, this is what you came here for, so you'd better do something!

➤ IF YOU PUSH THE BUTTONS ONE AT A TIME FROM LEFT TO RIGHT, TURN TO PAGE 139

➤ IF YOU PUSH ALL THE BUTTONS AT THE SAME TIME, TURN TO PAGE 140

➤ IF YOU TRY TO FIGURE OUT A CERTAIN SEQUENCE TO PUSH THE BUTTONS IN, TURN TO PAGE 141

Okay, let's not overthink this, you think.

Or maybe you *should* overthink it?

This place has been making you question everything and second-guess yourself at almost every step, but sometimes you need to follow your instincts and use common sense. That's why they hired you, isn't it?

Isn't it?

In all your years with Fazbear Entertainment, they haven't exactly had people lining up to fill positions, and it's been harder and harder to hire new staff, thanks to negative news coverage of a few isolated incidents. You were so proud when they hired you for security, but what if you were the only candidate?

Well, you've proven your value time and time again. Tonight is no different. You're going to leave Freddy's with a spotless record and a glowing recommendation, so you'll have your pick of opportunities—a job that will give you more time to spend with Coppelia.

And a lower chance of suffering serious harm, disability, or death on the job.

You quickly press each button on the panel in sequence. They glow crimson and a soft hum indicates power shutting off around the restaurant. Then, one by one, the buttons turn green again as the system resets.

You quietly crack open the door to peek into the Dining Area. The main lights are now out.

➤ IF YOU SNEAK THROUGH THE DARK RESTAURANT TO THE SECURITY OFFICE, TURN TO PAGE 154

➤ IF YOU TAKE THE VENTS BACK TO THE SECURITY OFFICE, TURN TO PAGE 142

The buttons are close enough together that you can just about push them all at the same time. That could be a kind of fail-safe, you reason, because there's no way someone would do that by accident, but it would be easy to push the buttons one at a time.

You place your left thumb against the first button and spread the fingertips of your right hand over the remaining four buttons. You feel something like a tingle or tickle in your hands, and the buttons hum at your touch. The hair on your head lifts away as if charged with static.

"Here goes," you say.

You push all five buttons simultaneously and the panel starts sparking. The buttons flash and start to scald your skin, but you can't pull your hands away—your muscles are locked as 1.21 gigawatts of power pump through you, your hands completing a big electrical circuit.

You smell something like cooking bacon and burnt hair, and then it's lights out—for you!

GAME OVER

➤ TO START FROM THE BEGINNING, TURN TO PAGE 2
➤ TO TRY THIS NIGHT AGAIN, TURN TO PAGE 121

Nothing is as it seems at Freddy Fazbear's Pizza. There must be a trick to this, or this is all a trick. You stare at the glowing buttons on the control panel. The metal around them is scratched. These faint lines could be numbers telling you what order to press the buttons in . . .

You rub your eyes. This place is getting to you. You look around for other clues. There's a faded poster of Bonnie on the back of the door—the intended way to enter and leave this room.

That could be significant. Why would someone put a mascot poster in here? Only staff would ever come to the Breaker Room. In big bright letters, the poster reads PARTY TIME! but the word *Time* is scratched out.

You've played enough point-and-click adventure games to realize this might be a hint. You need to press these buttons to shut *down* the partying.

Wait, there are five buttons, and five letters in the word *party*. P-A-R-T-Y. What if each button is one letter, and you need to press them in alphabetical order?

So the second button would be first, because it's P. You press it and the light changes from green to red. Now A is next. You push the first button.

You're so certain you're on to something, you miss Freddy entering the room—to shut *you* down!

GAME OVER

> TO START FROM THE BEGINNING, TURN TO PAGE 2
> TO TRY THIS NIGHT AGAIN, TURN TO PAGE 121

It would be faster to take a more direct route back to the Security Office, but strange enough, you feel more comfortable in the ventilation shaft. It's the only way to travel!

The trip doesn't take you as long as you thought it would, since you know the way now. Once you thought you heard something scraping and clanking and thumping in the vents, but it was pretty far away, off near Pirate Cove.

"It's almost six a.m., Foxy," you call out softly. While you doubt he heard you or would listen if he did, for some reason, he does not come after you.

When you crawl out of the vent into the Security Office, you see that the clock reads 5:57 a.m. It's close to quitting time.

➤ WAIT FOR 6:00 A.M. AND HEAD HOME ON PAGE 240

You really didn't think this through. To get from the West Hall corridor to the right side of the Dining Area, you have to either sneak along the back of the Dining Area or go back and cut across the Security Office to the East Hall.

Rather than waste any more time, you decide to take your chances where you are.

Just keep dancing, you think.

With all the lights on, the animatronics notice you right away, and they are delighted to have an audience. You barely make it halfway across the room before Bonnie snatches you up.

They give you the best seat in the house at the front of the Dining Area. It gives you a perfect view of the stage, where Freddy, Bonnie, and Chica perform increasingly disturbing songs and dance routines. You have no choice but to watch and hope that their batteries wear down eventually—and try not to think about what they'll do with you when they get bored.

GAME OVER

➤ TO START FROM THE BEGINNING, TURN TO PAGE 2

➤ TO TRY THIS NIGHT AGAIN, TURN TO PAGE 121

You're already on the left side of the Dining Area, so it's a shorter trip to the north end of it—and you want to spend as little time in here with the animatronics as you can.

You crawl along, keeping behind the tables and out of their line of sight. But there's a big gap between the tables near Pirate Cove. They don't want anyone sitting too close to the entrance.

You keep an eye on Freddy, Foxy, Bonnie, and Chica. When their attention is elsewhere, you sprint toward the next table. When you're halfway across, the music abruptly stops. You instinctively dive-roll to your left—through the curtains into the dark entrance of Pirate Cove.

You bruise your shoulder, but that likely hurts less than being forced to occupy the same space as an exoskeleton in a mascot suit.

The animatronics didn't see you. They're still going about their business. Another song starts up, playing backward. "Misery" . . . "Agony" . . .

But for how long?

You might be trapped in Pirate Cove for a while, waiting for your chance to move forward. But this is also a rare opportunity: You've never been back here before, and with Foxy enjoying his comeback tour with the old band, you can look around this area while he's gone. Maybe there's another way to the Breaker Room through here.

➤ IF YOU LOOK AROUND PIRATE COVE, TURN TO PAGE 146
➤ IF YOU PEEK THROUGH THE CURTAINS TO SEE IF IT'S SAFE, TURN TO PAGE 148

You crouch-run toward the party table closest to the West Hall entrance. Chica swivels her head in your direction, but you drop flat to the floor before she spots you.

You squeeze between two chairs to get under the table and wince when one of them scrapes along the tile. It turns out the cleaning crew doesn't do a great job under tables. The tiles are sticky and crumbs dig into the palms of your hands as you crawl across them. You encounter a slice of petrified pizza that almost makes you gag.

Then there's the pile of small bones you happen across. The restaurant's chicken wings are boneless, so you don't know what these could be.

This is so disgusting. You've come to realize that not everyone has been as diligent at their work as you, and you wonder what other corners are being cut around here.

You're about to cross to an adjoining table when it suddenly tips over. You dart back out of sight and scurry to get under another table just as the one you leave is tipped away. Bonnie smashes his guitar down inches from where your head was a moment ago.

Bonnie and Chica are destroying the Dining Area, and there are only so many tables to hide under.

They have found a new game to play: Whack-a-Ralph!

GAME OVER

➤ TO START FROM THE BEGINNING, TURN TO PAGE 2
➤ TO TRY THIS NIGHT AGAIN, TURN TO PAGE 121

As you look around Pirate Cove, you consider why you've never been back here before, even during the day. The only reason you can come up with is Foxy makes you uncomfortable.

You used to love watching him perform, and as a lifelong fan of pirate stories, he was always your favorite of the Fazbear mascots. But seeing him up close and personal was a different story, and you have to admit, he's scary, especially in his current state of disrepair.

Especially when you know what the animatronics are truly capable of. You just never want to be alone with Foxy in a room, especially on his home turf.

➤ TURN TO PAGE 147

It's a shame they had to shut this area down, though. It was popular with the kids, and you can tell the designers put a lot of work into it. They built a veritable cave of wonders, with treasure chests and glittering piles of gold and jewels around Foxy's charging platform. They're all fake, of course, but they're so convincing, you want to stuff your pockets with them.

They really should pay us more, you think. *But just remember what happened in* The Goonies.

At the very back of the Cove, you find a nook with a pedestal and an old-fashioned scale: a beam with pans suspended at either end. The pans are filled with gold and trinkets. The pan on the left is slightly lower than the one on the right. There is a small slot in the pedestal just below the scale, like the ones that dispense tickets at games around Freddy Fazbear's Pizza.

Below the alcove is a metal grate covering a ventilation shaft.

> IF YOU EXAMINE THE GRATE, TURN TO PAGE 149
> IF YOU TAKE SOME COINS FROM THE LEFT PAN, TURN TO PAGE 150
> IF YOU HAVE A <u>COIN</u> AND WANT TO ADD IT TO THE RIGHT PAN, TURN TO PAGE 151
> IF YOU HAVE A <u>RING</u> AND WANT TO ADD IT TO THE RIGHT PAN, TURN TO PAGE 152

You peer out from between the curtains. Freddy, Bonnie, and Chica are still partying, but Foxy is looking right at you.

You're afraid to move, certain that the slightest motion will send him running toward you. You don't even dare blink.

The irony of the situation doesn't escape you: You and Foxy on opposite sides of his curtain, watching and waiting for your chance to move.

I guess that makes this "the irony curtain," you think.

You snicker at your own terrible joke and Foxy tenses, ready to spring into action. You freeze. No more bad puns!

This isn't how you thought it would end, in a staring contest with an animatronic. You consider that if he runs out of power while sitting there with his eyes open, you would never realize it.

Not being able to move your body is sending your mind racing, and you can't stop from thinking about everything: your life, your daughter, the choices that brought you here. You can't control the thoughts that pop into your head.

The only thing you know for sure—

Stop, you warn yourself, but you can't keep the punch line from coming:

Never play chicken with a fox.

You laugh.

GAME OVER

➤ TO START FROM THE BEGINNING, TURN TO PAGE 2
➤ TO TRY THIS NIGHT AGAIN, TURN TO PAGE 121

The vent under the prize scale would make a great hiding spot. In fact, you could even use the ventilation shaft to crawl to the Breaker Room without being detected by the animatronics.

You stoop to examine the grate covering the vent. It's secured by four big screws in each corner. Someone was serious about limiting Foxy's access to the rest of the pizza place, or preventing someone in the vents from accidentally crawling into his lair. Unfortunately, it's also preventing you from escaping through the ventilation shaft.

Footsteps approach. You have to get through that grate right now!

➤ IF YOU TRY TO PULL THE GRATE OFF, TURN TO PAGE 155
➤ IF YOU HAVE A SCREWDRIVER, USE IT ON PAGE 156

You take a coin from the scale pan on the left and are disappointed to discover it isn't real. It's lightweight and plastic, painted gold with Foxy's face on it.

It's worthless except as a souvenir for your daughter. You slip the coin into your pocket and then remove more of the plastic coins from the left pan, making it rise until it's at the same level as the one on the right.

Once the scale is in balance, you turn around and find Foxy standing behind you, head tilted sideways. He raises his right arm, with the wicked-looking hook on the end of it.

Whatever happens next, you feel like you earned it by stealing from your job.

GAME OVER

➤ TO START FROM THE BEGINNING, TURN TO PAGE 2
➤ TO TRY THIS NIGHT AGAIN, TURN TO PAGE 121

You reach into your pocket and pull out the coin with Foxy's face that you found on your second night. Of course! It belongs here.

You carefully place the coin on top of the mound of coins and plastic gems in the pan on the right.

Nothing happens. The plastic coin barely adds any weight to the pan and the scale doesn't shift at all. You wonder if you could just nudge it with your finger. It's not like a boulder is going to chase you if you mess with the balance.

But an alarm might go off, and that could bring something worse. You can always outrace a boulder, but not Foxy.

If you don't have anything heavy to put on the right pan, maybe you need to take coins away from the one on the left.

➤ IF YOU TAKE SOME COINS FROM THE LEFT PAN, TURN TO PAGE 150
➤ IF YOU HAVE A <u>RING</u> AND ADD IT TO THE RIGHT PAN, TURN TO PAGE 152
➤ IF YOU CONTINUE ON TO THE BREAKER ROOM, TURN TO PAGE 153

You need something heavy to weigh down the pan on the right. You reach into your pocket and pull out the gold ring you found in the Kitchen.

As soon as you add it to the lighter pan, the scale shifts into perfect balance. A recording of cheering children plays, confetti falls, and the pedestal dispenses a ticket.

"That's it? One lousy ticket?" you mutter. The gold ring was definitely worth more than whatever you can get with this at the Prize Counter. What a rip-off.

You consider grabbing the ring back, but you've always been one to play by the rules, and that includes not cheating at games. So you take the ticket.

It's an old ticket, wrinkled and stained with drops of . . . tomato sauce. The green color has faded, along with the words stamped on it: FREDBEAR'S FAMILY DINER. Now that's a throwback! That place has been closed for years, but it was a predecessor to Fazbear Entertainment's Freddy's Pizza franchise. This artifact might just be worth more than the gold ring if you found the right buyer. Freddy's biggest fans will buy anything!

Then you turn the ticket over and the dollar signs fade away. Someone's written on the back of it, and the ink looks recent: 2-0-1-4.

Are those footsteps? You might have company soon.

> ADD THE TICKET TO YOUR INVENTORY
> IF YOU PEEK THROUGH THE CURTAIN, TURN TO PAGE 148
> IF YOU LOOK FOR SOMEPLACE TO HIDE, TURN TO PAGE 149

What are you doing? You don't have time to play games! You have to get to the Breaker Room to stop the animatronics' party.

You sneak back to the curtain and peek out. What you see makes your blood run cold.

From their various positions throughout the Dining Area, Freddy, Chica, and Foxy are all watching the entrance to Pirate Cove. They see you!

You panic and close the curtains, as if they could stop a three-hundred-pound-plus animatronic from getting inside.

You back up from the entrance, frantically looking for a place to hide.

Then you come to a terrible realization: *Bonnie wasn't in the Dining Area.*

Something crashes behind you. You turn and see a mangled metal grate on the floor—and Bonnie, crawling out of a vent in the back wall.

GAME OVER

➤ TO START FROM THE BEGINNING, TURN TO PAGE 2
➤ TO TRY THIS NIGHT AGAIN, TURN TO PAGE 121

You sneak into the dark Dining Area. You successfully stopped the animatronics before they did any real damage. The morning crew shouldn't have any trouble straightening the askew tables and righting all the chairs. They'll be curious about what happened, and they'll probably blame you, but this whole incident will be in your report.

Not that anyone ever reads your reports, or believes what you wrote. The home office doesn't like paper trails, so they're probably filing your paperwork right into the trash can.

Freddy, Bonnie, and Chica have returned to the stage and are recharging on their platforms. As you expected, switching off the lights triggered their Night Mode. Their internal clocks are probably all confused now, and they'll likely be low on power tomorrow. But even if they freeze up on the stage, it will be far from the worst thing that has happened during a performance.

By a long shot.

You have nearly reached the Security Office and are feeling pretty good about the night's work when you hear heavy footsteps running behind you—the clank of bare metal feet against a tiled floor.

You break into a run without even looking behind you.

Though you never see what hits you, it has to be Foxy. Since he's been taken out of the limelight, he responds differently to darkness. And this is how *he* likes to party.

GAME OVER

➤ TO START FROM THE BEGINNING, TURN TO PAGE 2
➤ TO TRY THIS NIGHT AGAIN, TURN TO PAGE 121

You grab onto the vent cover and pull as hard as you can. The sharp edges slice into the tips of your fingers, but you don't let that stop you.

The screws are old and the grate slowly wiggles free. If you can loosen it just a little more, you should be able to twist off the screws manually with just your fingers. Who needs a stinking screwdriver?

You're making so much noise, though, and the footsteps nearby quicken and grow louder. You also hear something in the ventilation shaft.

Thump, thump, thump.

You think it's just your exertions echoing back to you, until a face suddenly appears pressed up against the metal grate.

Bonnie!

He pushes at the vent, and now that you've loosened it for him, it pops right off.

You scramble backward on the floor until you bump into something hard. You reach behind you and feel exposed endoskeletal feet. In the corner of your eye, you see the flash of a metal hook.

GAME OVER

➤ TO START FROM THE BEGINNING, TURN TO PAGE 2
➤ TO TRY THIS NIGHT AGAIN, TURN TO PAGE 121

Having the right tool for the right job makes such a difference! The screwdriver makes quick work of removing the screws from the vent cover. You pull it off quietly and climb inside the shaft, just as something enters Pirate Cove.

From inside the shaft, you see Foxy's feet as he stomps around, looking for you. He stops right in front of the vent opening and studies the scale for a while. You hear a crash, and the scale and toy treasures on it scatter across the floor. Finally, he walks away and out of Pirate Cove, singing a little ditty.

You wipe sweat from your face and take stock of your choices. You think if you turn left, the shaft will lead you back to the Security Office. Which means right should lead toward the stage and the Breaker Room.

➤ HEAD TOWARD THE BREAKER ROOM ON PAGE 157

Bruce Willis makes this look easy, you think as you crawl through the ventilation shaft on your hands and knees. The metal is caked in old grease that must have been carried here from the Kitchen over the years. Cobwebs cling to your face and hair. Warm air pushes past your face, and you smell something that is definitely dead and rotting.

Probably a small animal, you think.

Each time you move, the metal flexes and wobbles and makes a soft *fwump*. Sound carries, and you're worried the animatronics will hear you if the music stops. Right now, there's no chance of being detected over the circus music they're blasting in the Dining Area. It's so loud, you feel the bass in the ventilation shaft.

You forge ahead. At least the shaft isn't as cramped as you would have expected—it's probably much bigger than it needs to be. Even Bonnie could probably fit inside.

Great. Now you're worrying about Bonnie coming after you in the vents.

There's no reason to assume they even know about the vents, you think. This is probably the safest place in the whole restaurant, other than the Security Office.

So why do the four close walls remind you of a coffin?

The Breaker Room can't be much farther. You reach a corridor branching to your right. Now which way do you go?

➤ IF YOU LISTEN FOR CLUES AS TO WHERE YOU ARE, TURN TO PAGE 132
➤ IF YOU HEAD TO THE RIGHT, TURN TO PAGE 133
➤ IF YOU KEEP MOVING FORWARD, TURN TO PAGE 134

Night 5—12:00 a.m.

You start your last shift ever at Freddy Fazbear's Pizza with mixed emotions. This has been a killer week, but you handled everything well, and the events of the last four nights have reminded you that you're still very good at your job. The animatronics require—no, they *deserve*—caretakers who appreciate them and understand them, and you've always been that.

And yet, you can certainly do without the high stress and anxiety that you might not survive until morning. Your daughter needs someone to take care of her, too. The night watchman can always be replaced, but she only has one dad.

Okay, technically fathers *can* be replaced, but there is definitely only one Coppelia, and you'd like to be in her life as she grows up. That's what all this is for, so you can get a job with a lower mortality rate and a better work-life balance.

For some reason, you've had a hard time remembering each night after you go home, until you come back to work the next day. Like it says in your Employee Handbook: *What happens at Freddy's stays at Freddy's* . . . unless there's major coverage in the papers and nightly news.

➤ TURN TO PAGE 159

One of the drawbacks of working the late shift is there are no coworkers to see you off on your last night. You always thought if you left this job, the company would throw you a big going-away party celebrating your many years of service.

Then again, considering what can happen at Freddy Fazbear's Pizza parties, you're probably better off not drawing too much attention to yourself—as sweet as it would be to hear Freddy sing "For He's a Jolly Good Fellow" to you.

Actually, it turns out the restaurant didn't even open today. You don't know why. Maybe it was because the Dining Area was such a mess, you think guiltily. That doesn't affect your shift, though, except who knows what the animatronics have been up to all day on their own?

Which reminds you about the job you have to do. This is no time to fall asleep at the wheel.

You switch on the monitor and check out the Show Stage camera. Your seat isn't even warm yet before you jump up from it in surprise— the stage is empty!

It's just after midnight—the animatronics are way ahead of schedule. They could be restless after being alone all day. Hopefully, they aren't upset about their party last night being interrupted. They might be out seeking revenge.

➤ TURN TO PAGE 160

Or could they be angry that you're leaving? You've been a part of the Fazbear Family™ for so long, perhaps they don't want you to go.

Or they don't want you to get away.

You laugh off these ridiculous notions as you punch buttons to check each camera. You've definitely been working here too long if you think the animatronics have a vendetta. They can only respond to external stimuli according to their programming, like recharging when the lights go out or restoring wandering exoskeletons to their suits where they belong.

Ha ha.

Ha.

You find the animatronics immediately. Bonnie is at the far end of the West Hall, heading toward the Security Office.

Freddy is in the Dining Area, making his way down the aisle toward the Security Office.

Foxy is halfway through the curtains of Pirate Cove—also probably on his way to the Security Office.

Who told them you're leaving? How do they know?

You swallow your panic and keep clicking around. Chica? Where's Chica?

The Kitchen camera is dark as usual, but you don't hear anyone in there. Chica could be anywhere.

You glance over at the open door to your right.

She could be anywhere.

> IF YOU CLOSE THE LEFT DOOR, TURN TO PAGE 161
> IF YOU CLOSE THE RIGHT DOOR, TURN TO PAGE 162
> IF YOU LISTEN TO THE KITCHEN FEED A LITTLE LONGER, TURN TO PAGE 163
> IF YOU CHECK THE VENTS BEHIND YOU, TURN TO PAGE 173

You know Bonnie's moving at a good clip down the hallway, so you rush over to the entrance on your left and slap the button that lowers the heavy door.

There. Good luck getting through that, you wascally wabbit.

You head back to your seat but draw up short because Chica is standing across from you, framed in the other doorway.

That is a big chicken, you think. Somehow she seems larger in person, when she isn't up on a stage, and she's on the verge of killing you.

This is probably the end for you, unless you happen to be carrying something that could save your life, for at least a few more minutes.

➤ **IF YOU HAVE <u>MR. CUPCAKE</u>, YOU MAY USE IT ON PAGE 164**
➤ **IF YOU HAVE A <u>WATER PISTOL</u>, YOU MAY USE IT ON PAGE 165**
➤ **IF YOU HAVE A <u>FLASHLIGHT</u>, YOU MAY USE IT ON PAGE 166**
➤ **IF YOU ARE EMPTY-HANDED OR DON'T WANT TO USE ANYTHING IN YOUR INVENTORY, TURN TO PAGE 167**

In the pit of your stomach, you feel certain that Chica is about to breach the Security Office, so you shut the door on your right—just in time! Someone bangs on the reinforced steel from the other side.

"'Tis some visitor,'" you mutter, "'tapping at my chamber door. Only this and nothing more.'" You flip on the hall light and see the distinctive shape of Chica. She keeps pounding on the door and shrieks.

"Quoth the chicken, 'Nevermore.'" You laugh shakily.

You often crack jokes when you're nervous, but this close call has got your pulse going. At least you know where all the animatronics are now—or where they were a few minutes ago. A lot could have changed already.

Last you checked, Bonnie was on his way down the West Hall to mess up your night. But you don't hear him now. He could still be lurking nearby, or maybe he's lost interest in you.

➤ IF YOU CHECK THE CAMERAS AGAIN, TURN TO PAGE 171

➤ IF YOU CLOSE THE LEFT DOOR, TURN TO PAGE 172

➤ IF YOU CHECK THE VENT, TURN TO PAGE 173

You switch back to the audio feed from the Kitchen and crank the volume on the monitor, leaning closer to the speakers. You hear the hiss of air over the microphone, the hum of the TV, and static crackling. It's as quiet as it—

Wait! Something is rustling, moving about. Then you hear a raspy sound that's almost human. It makes moaning, guttural attempts at speech.

Weird. Usually, Chica just knocks some pots and pans around in there. Is she trying to tell you something?

You lower the volume on the monitor. But you still hear the sounds as clearly as if they were coming from right behind you.

Your skin crawls. You switch off the monitor, and in the darkened glass is the distorted reflection of Chica standing over your right shoulder.

She opens her mouth and the airy sound she makes could be the word *Hell*.

Oh. She's saying "hello." In the creepiest way imaginable.

The monitor reflects back the utter fear on your face—and the instant Chica grabs you.

GAME OVER

➤ TO START FROM THE BEGINNING, TURN TO PAGE 2
➤ TO TRY THIS NIGHT AGAIN, TURN TO PAGE 158

The only thing you can come up with is Mr. Cupcake, Chica's iconic prop. Her eyes lock on to it and she extends a grasping hand.

Bingo!

You're glad you didn't give this presumably useless toy to your daughter, though she would have loved to have it on her shelf and it makes a nice memento of your time working at Freddy's. This might be the only thing that can save you from the voracious chicken.

Now that you have her attention, what do you do with the cupcake?

➤ IF YOU THROW IT AT CHICA, TURN TO PAGE 168

➤ IF YOU THROW IT INTO THE EAST HALL, TURN TO PAGE 169

➤ IF YOU THROW IT INTO THE OPEN VENT, TURN TO PAGE 170

You draw your water pistol, aim, and fire at Chica.

A stream of water arcs from the plastic toy and splashes harmlessly against her LET'S EAT bib.

"Huh," you say. "I should have expected that."

You pump the trigger of the water pistol, showering Chica with droplets, but it's not enough water to affect anything but her mood—and the security TV. Electronics sizzle and pop, and smoke wisps out of the chassis. The air smells like burnt ozone.

Now you can't keep an eye on the other animatronics, but that's okay because you have one right in front of you, and she is demanding all of your attention in the little time you have left.

GAME OVER

➤ TO START FROM THE BEGINNING, TURN TO PAGE 2
➤ TO TRY THIS NIGHT AGAIN, TURN TO PAGE 158

You fumble around in your pockets for anything useful and come up with the flashlight.

In the aftermath of "The Bite of '87," staff spread tips around the restaurant of how to slow or stop the animatronics if they ever attacked again. You put a stop to those harmful rumors, once again earning the title of Employee of the Month. That time, the prize was a special pizza named after you for thirty days. It proved unpopular and only lasted four days, though; it turns out no one wanted to buy a pizza named "The Ralph," covered in anchovies and artichokes.

You don't really blame anyone. You can still taste that monstrosity.

One of the survival strategies suggested at the time was shining a bright light into the animatronics' eyes to disorient them and temporarily lock them in position until they reset their sensors and recalibrated their programming.

You slide the button forward on the flashlight and aim the beam directly into Chica's eyes.

That little trick might work on another animatronic, but Chica *loves* being in the spotlight. And she's about to make you part of a show you will never forget.

GAME OVER

➤ TO START FROM THE BEGINNING, TURN TO PAGE 2
➤ TO TRY THIS NIGHT AGAIN, TURN TO PAGE 158

You grab your desk chair and shove it at Chica to slow her down, then punch the button behind you to open the door. With any luck, Bonnie hasn't made it all the way down the hall yet, and you can hide in the Supply Closet until help comes in the morning.

You almost trip over your own feet getting out of the office, but it seems you've used up all your luck this week. Bonnie is blocking your access to the closet.

You back up into the West Hall corner. Bonnie slowly advances toward you: *Thump. Thump. Thump.*

You giggle madly as a stray thought short-circuits your fight-or-flight reflexes: *Thumper would have been a better name for him.* But Fazbear Entertainment was already in enough legal trouble without the additional headache of fighting copyright law.

Chica watches you from the West Hall door, inside the Security Office.

To avoid looking at either of the animatronics keeping you cornered, you stare at the poster of Freddy Fazbear on the wall. It should read LET'S PARTY! but instead, Freddy is ripping his own head off.

Why would he do that? you wonder.

Strong, plush hands settle on both sides of your head. The joints in your neck pop—

GAME OVER

➤ TO START FROM THE BEGINNING, TURN TO PAGE 2
➤ TO TRY THIS NIGHT AGAIN, TURN TO PAGE 158

Chica takes a step toward you, still reaching for her prop. The sudden motion startles and frightens you, and you nearly fumble Mr. Cupcake.

You catch it before it falls, juggle it between your hands a few times like a hot potato, and then toss it in Chica's direction.

"Stay frosty!" you shout.

You probably thought she would catch it and then turn and leave, but instead the toy bounces off her bib and tumbles to the floor. It rolls out of sight under the desk.

Chica's expression becomes an angry frown. When she opens her mouth, she hisses static and garbled, terrifying sounds stream from her beak with human teeth.

Something latches painfully onto your leg. You look down, and Mr. Cupcake has glomped onto your calf and is biting down hard. Blood squirts and sprays everywhere—he's chewing through an artery. Your leg starts to feel cold.

You kick vigorously to try to shake Mr. Cupcake off and then try to pry him from the leg with your hands, but he won't let go. You're losing blood fast, which only makes you weaker.

The room spins. You lurch, stumble, and fall. You drift in and out of consciousness as Chica grabs Mr. Cupcake and leaves the Security Office, dragging you along with it by the leg. It seems the two of you are now inseparable—until death do you part.

GAME OVER

➤ TO START FROM THE BEGINNING, TURN TO PAGE 2
➤ TO TRY THIS NIGHT AGAIN, TURN TO PAGE 158

You have only one hope. You can't get away from Chica, so you need *her* to get away from *you*.

You wind up your arm like a pitcher on the baseball mound, and you throw Mr. Cupcake past Chica and into the East Hall behind her.

She glares at you before turning and following her faithful prop out of the Security Office. As soon as she's gone, you jump toward the button by the door and slam the palm of your hand into it. The door *whooshes* and *clangs*, dropping down and locking the animatronics out.

Or, if you look at it another way, the door is locking you inside.

You flip on the light in the east corridor and watch Chica's shadow move away from the office. It sounds like the cupcake is hopping away and she hurries to catch up to it, footsteps thudding and echoing down the corridor.

You wipe sweat from your forehead. *Thank you, Mr. Cupcake.*

You listen at the left door. It sounds quiet, so you open the door and look out. No sign of Bonnie. But he's probably close by, perhaps seeking another way inside.

➤ IF YOU CHECK THE CAMERAS AGAIN, TURN TO PAGE 171
➤ IF YOU CHECK THE VENT, TURN TO PAGE 190

You maintain eye contact with Chica as you toss Mr. Cupcake into the vent to your right. The toy bounces around in the metal shaft. Chica becomes enraged and she rushes at you, screaming.

At the same time, Mr. Cupcake sails through the air and lands on the floor between you. Chica staggers to a halt and the two of you stare down at the object. Something has taken a big bite out of the top of it, exposing electronics inside its rubbery outer layer.

You turn toward the vent and squint to see what or who is inside. Meanwhile, Chica backs up and leaves the office with the deformed Mr. Cupcake.

What could have scared Chica away? you wonder in horror.

You decide to beat a hasty retreat as well, but before you even have your coat on, loud knocking emanates from the ventilation shaft. You crouch to get a better look at the inside.

You see two glowing white eyes. Then a wide, grinning mouth that is ready to take a bite out of you.

GAME OVER

➤ TO START FROM THE BEGINNING, TURN TO PAGE 2
➤ TO TRY THIS NIGHT AGAIN, TURN TO PAGE 158

You pull up the camera for the West Hall to check on Bonnie's progress, but he isn't your main concern anymore—because Foxy is racing toward the Security Office!

You jump up to close the left door to block Foxy, but his footsteps are loud and fast in the hall. He could reach the door before you can shut it. Act fast!

> **IF YOU CLOSE THE LEFT DOOR AGAIN, TURN TO PAGE 172**
> **IF YOU HIDE IN THE VENT, TURN TO PAGE 174**
> **IF YOU HAVE A <u>WATER PISTOL</u>, YOU MAY USE IT ON PAGE 176**

You leap toward the button beside the left door and slam your palm against it hard, as if more force will make it close faster. As soon as the reinforced barricade falls into place, you hear a frustrated scream and heavy fists against the metal. The door shakes in the frame and vibrates with each impact, but it holds.

You got to that in the nick of time, but movement in the corner of your eye makes you think you still weren't quick enough. Bonnie's face appears at the vent. He tilts his head from side to side and stares at you.

You're surrounded, with no way out and little hope of surviving until morning.

➤ IF YOU TRY TO CLOSE THE VENT, TURN TO PAGE 175
➤ IF YOU HAVE A <u>FLASHLIGHT</u>, YOU MAY USE IT ON PAGE 177
➤ IF YOU TRY TO DEFEND YOURSELF, TURN TO PAGE 178

Now that you know the vent is there, you hate having an open access point behind your back. You'll feel much better knowing that it's secured, so you scramble to the rear wall of the Security Office and crouch down in front of the low rectangular opening.

It's dark.

You sigh and get down on your hands and knees so you can poke your head into the vent. You look to your right and squint, but you can't see into the depths of the shaft. You also don't hear anything but the soft whoosh of circulating air. It seems safe enough. Maybe the animatronics don't know about this path to the office.

You retreat from the space and climb to your feet, dusting off your hands and pants. You turn and your blood turns to ice: Bonnie stands at the left door and Chica is at the right. They look at each other, then slowly turn their heads to focus on you.

You drop to the ground and try to escape into the vent, but strong hands grab your legs and yank you backward. Bonnie and Chica pull your legs in opposite directions, like when you and your daughter break the turkey's wishbone at Thanksgiving.

"I wish—"

Snap!

GAME OVER

➤ TO START FROM THE BEGINNING, TURN TO PAGE 2

➤ TO TRY THIS NIGHT AGAIN, TURN TO PAGE 158

You run and dive for the open vent at the back of the Security Office and quickly worm your way inside. You turn around and press yourself flat against the cold metal floor, peering out and trying to control your breathing to make as little noise as possible.

Foxy bursts into the office and looks around wildly for you, his eyes burning white in the dimly lit room. He opens the right door, allowing Chica to enter the office, and together the two of them study the TV. They push buttons to check the different cameras around the facility. To check for *you*.

The sight of the animatronics working together, operating technology, gives you a sick feeling in your stomach. This is more than a fluke in their programming, some faulty logic loop. They're acting strategically with intent.

And that intent is to murder you.

Your breathing is shallow and you're drenched in cold sweat. This is bad.

But it gets worse when you hear moaning on your left, echoing down the ventilation shaft. Foxy and Chica hear it, too, and they're coming to investigate.

Shaking, knowing this is the end, you turn to the left. Tears obscure your vision, but you see a large, blue blob crawling toward you.

GAME OVER

➤ TO START FROM THE BEGINNING, TURN TO PAGE 2
➤ TO TRY THIS NIGHT AGAIN, TURN TO PAGE 158

You make a desperate rush to reach the button that will block off the vent. Boosted by adrenaline and your sheer will to survive, you make it there before Bonnie exits the vent. You slap the button in relief.

The lights flicker and electricity buzzes, but the ventilation cover doesn't drop.

You frantically hit the button again and again, but nothing happens. The red light behind the translucent button dims. You glance at the two closed doors behind you.

There's a reason the vent was open—it appears not enough power has been allocated to the Security Office to activate both doors and the ventilation cover at the same time. You'll have to choose to open one of the doors in order to divert some juice to power this one.

Alas, Bonnie has other plans. He crawls out of the vent, head rotated sickeningly to look at you from the side. He opens his mouth to emit a low, murderous chuckle.

GAME OVER

➤ TO START FROM THE BEGINNING, TURN TO PAGE 2
➤ TO TRY THIS NIGHT AGAIN, TURN TO PAGE 158

All you have is a water pistol, so you draw it and take a defensive stance, just like you practiced in the mirror after watching the *Lethal Weapon* movies. This child's toy is far from lethal, but it makes you feel better, and you hope that Foxy doesn't recognize that it's harmless.

Foxy bursts into the office and wastes no time rushing at you. Even though you knew he was coming, his sudden, aggressive appearance startles you, and you reflexively fire your gun at his chest.

Water squirts from the pistol into a tear in Foxy's mascot suit that exposes the exoskeleton within. Shockingly, the water sizzles, and sparks shoot out of the chest cavity. Foxy jerks and stutters to a stop, his hook and exposed metal hand just inches from your neck. The acrid smell of cooked electronics reaches your nostrils.

The light in Foxy's eyes dies, and for a moment regret overwhelms you. You wish it hadn't come to this. He's down for the count, for now. But there's no time for a eulogy—you brush past him and hurry to the back of the Security Office. You punch the button to close the ventilation cover, and a metal grate *kerthunks* into place. Not a moment too soon—something is moving around inside the ventilation shaft.

But now you hear strains of classical music. You sigh.

Freddy Fazbear is on his way.

➤ CHECK THE MONITORS TO FIND FREDDY ON PAGE 179
➤ IF YOU HAVE THE BONUS ITEM, YOU MAY USE IT ON PAGE 183

You pull out your flashlight and hold it in front of you with both hands. You press the button to turn it on, and a bright beam of white light cuts through the darkness. You shine it directly into Bonnie's face.

He flinches and pulls back. His eyes blink, one at a time. Left, then right. Left, then right. It's creepy. His servos whir and his jaw stutters open and closed, but he can't seem to move.

You switch off the flashlight, and his eyes roll a few times before he recovers. He opens his mouth and screams—

The cry is cut off as you turn the flashlight back on again. He makes a horrible gasping sound that repeats over and over again like a stuck record.

"Okay." You breathe. Your hands shake a bit and the beam wavers, but you hold it on Bonnie's eyes. The light must be causing an overload in his photoreceptors. The animatronics are all programmed to respond to the light levels, so they're in performance mode during the day, when the fluorescent lights are on in the restaurant. When it's dark, they recharge and roam. The bright light is confusing Bonnie, so he doesn't know what to do next.

For how long?

You hold the light and eye the clock. You just have to make it until morning.

The light flickers and dims until you whack the side of it with a palm. You wish you'd installed fresh batteries.

➤ WAIT OUT THE END OF YOUR SHIFT AND TURN TO PAGE 188

You refuse to go down without a fight. You have been dealing with these animatronics for four long nights, surviving by the skin of your teeth, and you are so, so tired. Tired of being hunted and terrified while you're just trying to do your job—trying to keep *them* safe.

Protecting Freddy, Bonnie, Chica, and Foxy is the prime directive for every Fazbear Entertainment employee. But you've already resigned. This is your last shift. From now on, your number one priority is keeping your daughter safe.

As Bonnie begins to emerge from the vent, you scream and run at him. Bonnie hesitates and looks up at you, his purple eyes wide and mouth slack. When you reach him, you pull back your right leg and kick him in the side of the head as hard as you can.

To your astonishment, Bonnie's head flies off. It hits a locker with a *crash*, then bounces and rolls under the desk.

"Wow," you say. "Someone must have done a bad job of attaching that."

Bonnie's body twitches, crawls forward a few steps, and then collapses. Electricity arcs from the torn wires dangling from its neck.

You did it. You're safe.

But not for much longer. You hear classical music coming toward the Security Office.

Freddy.

> ➤ IF YOU CHECK THE SECURITY CAMERAS, TURN TO PAGE 179
> ➤ IF YOU TRY TO CALL THE POLICE FOR HELP, TURN TO PAGE 193
> ➤ IF YOU HAVE THE BONUS ITEM, YOU MAY USE IT ON PAGE 183

You're an old pro at pushing buttons. You cycle through every camera in the restaurant at a record pace, looking for any sign of the restaurant's star mascot. It only takes you a quick glance to dismiss each location—until you get to the East Hall corner.

Freddy is standing there, and he is looking straight at the camera. His expression looks the same as ever, but somehow it seems more sinister.

His music continues playing, and this time you recognize it. You've been listening to classical music stations on your drives to and from work for the past few days, hoping it will come up. When it did, a sudden panic attack forced you to pull over to the side of the road until the song ended. But the DJ identified it as a song from the opera *Carmen*, about a bullfighter.

An interesting choice. Is that how Freddy sees himself? Or is it a challenge to the listener to stand up and fight?

You choose to fight. In this instance, it means locking your eyes on that monitor and watching Freddy. As long as you're looking at him and his song is playing, you don't think he will attack.

➤ TURN TO PAGE 180

It's a long night, watching Freddy, hoping that no one will sneak in through the vent and get you while you're preoccupied and essentially helpless. If the other animatronics are still waiting and lurking, they leave you alone—it's just you and Freddy. Your whole world is that small rectangular screen with the grainy image of a murderous animatronic bear in a top hat.

You blink as little as possible, though your eyes are burning and blurring with tears. It seems each time you do, the posters on the wall change. One moment, there's a list of restaurant rules behind Freddy; the next, it's a newspaper page showing a headline about missing children.

You want to read it, but you know the moment you shift your focus to anything other than Freddy, you'll be lost. But he keeps trying—you know it has to be Freddy's doing, whether he is somehow changing what's on the walls or merely your perception of them.

Blink. Now you're looking at sad, scary children's drawings that make you feel simultaneously vulnerable and malevolent as if you are both victim and perpetrator of some horrible crimes. This isn't who you truly are. It's this place.

➤ TURN TO PAGE 181

You feel like you're losing your mind. Freddy keeps trying to shake your attention. Now he seems to be shifting his position around the room, but it could just as easily be a camera glitch that makes him appear to teleport to different places. If he can do that, you fear he will somehow teleport into the Security Office, bypassing the closed doors.

You dare not look away from the screen, but it must be nearly 6:00 a.m. The night is almost at an end, and you're still alive. But you're eyes are weary from staring at the screen, and you worry you will never lose the image of Freddy—perhaps it is burned onto your retinas, burned into your very soul.

Just as you're sure a new day is dawning, you experience vertigo and have the sensation that you're disconnecting from your body. From reality.

You black out for a moment, and when you come to, you are in the west corner of the restaurant, staring up at the security camera.

What?

➤ TURN TO PAGE 182

You feel heavier somehow but also bigger and stronger and colder. You want to look down at your hands, to make sure you still have all your fingers. And that they're not covered in brown fur. And you still have organic bones, not a metal endoskeleton. But what if you look away from the camera and are stuck in this body forever?

I'm just hallucinating, you think. *This isn't real.*

I might be hallucinating and *this is real.*

When 6:00 a.m. rolls around, your shift is over and you head home, feeling both liberated from Freddy Fazbear's Pizza and as if you'll never really escape it. So much of your identity is caught up in that restaurant, it can't be that easy to let go.

You enter your house and look for Coppelia. She must still be asleep, so you go to her room to wake her up. The door creaks open and a lump under the bedcovers moves.

Her head pops out, hair a tangled mess as usual. She yawns big. Just as she is opening her eyes, you wonder if she will like the new you.

GAME OVER

➤ TO START FROM THE BEGINNING, TURN TO PAGE 2
➤ TO TRY THIS NIGHT AGAIN, TURN TO PAGE 158

You cannot wait for this night to end, preferably with you seeing the sun rise on your way home to your daughter. The likelihood of that scenario is decreasing by the second as you hear Freddy Fazbear's signature music draw closer. It seems to be coming through the open vent behind you.

You aren't even certain anymore that Freddy or the other animatronics obey the laws of reality. For all you know, he can just teleport into the office or anywhere else he wants to be in the blink of an eye. Maybe that's why he doesn't move around all that much. He doesn't have to.

With weary resignation, you pull out the mobile phone. What you do next may be the last thing you ever do.

➤ CALL FOR HELP ON PAGE 184
➤ CALL HOME ON PAGE 185
➤ RECORD A MESSAGE FOR YOUR REPLACEMENT ON PAGE 186

"9-1-1, what is your emergency?"

As quickly as you can, you tell the switchboard operator every-thing, and surprisingly she believes you. It might help that she can hear the animatronics banging against the door, Freddy's maniacal laughter, and the creepy circus music, punctuated by the sound of children crying.

"I always knew something was off about that restaurant, and I don't mean the cheese in the pizza. I don't know about killer animatronics, but it sounds like something is going down. I'm sending a squad car."

An animatronic in the hallway lets out a terrifying scream.

"I'll send *two* cars," she says. "Sit tight, sir. Help is on the way."

You are so relieved that she was able to hear everything happening right now—you were starting to think it was all in your head.

What if it *is* all in your head, even the 9-1-1 call? In that case, of course you heard what you wanted to hear.

Pretty soon you hear something else: police car sirens. A banging and crash as they beat down the door to get in. Gunshots. The cavalry has arrived.

You're saved and reunited with your daughter. Fazbear Entertainment can't fire you anymore, but they do sue you for defama-tion and destruction of private property.

Worst of all, you're never quite able to believe what you're seeing and hearing again. Part of you is convinced you're still in the restaurant and that it will never, ever let you leave.

GAME OVER

➤ TO START FROM THE BEGINNING, TURN TO PAGE 2
➤ TO TRY THIS NIGHT AGAIN, TURN TO PAGE 158

With a trembling finger, you dial your home number. It's early in the morning, and you hate to wake up your daughter, but you want to hear her voice. You need to let her know you would never abandon her.

The line clicks and Coppelia's groggy voice answers, "Yeah?"

"Is that how you answer the phone?" you say.

"Yeah. Dad? What time is it?"

"Late. Or early, depending on how you look at it."

"How's work? Are you coming home soon?"

"Oh, I wish."

"Is something wrong?" What can you say to her? There's so much, a lifetime of unwanted advice, family stories, bad jokes. But it all boils down to three words.

You abruptly notice that Foxy's eyes are glowing again. He has reactivated, but for some reason he hasn't attacked you.

Because he's listening.

You realize that it's quiet. Too quiet. The other animatronics have stopped their moaning and knocking. Even Freddy's music is silent.

"I *know*, Dad." You can practically hear her eyes rolling.

"I have to say it anyway, while I can." You take a deep breath. "Don't come here."

You disconnect the call and calmly erase your number from the history. You look up at Foxy.

"Promise to leave her alone and I'll stay. For good."

Foxy nods slowly, though it's not like you have a choice.

GAME OVER

➤ TO START FROM THE BEGINNING, TURN TO PAGE 2

➤ TO TRY THIS NIGHT AGAIN, TURN TO PAGE 158

It's looking like this is going to be your last night. It's some consolation that you will continue on in some way. Through your daughter, yes, but also through your legacy here at Freddy Fazbear's Pizza. You might even end up saving someone's life one day, through those recordings for the next person who will sit in this chair.

Whoever that poor soul may be.

Do you have any last words, maybe something that could help succeed where you failed?

Don't overthink it. You dial the number for the recording system and start talking.

"Hello, hello! Hey!"

You realize you never left a message for them last night. This will be sent on, what, their fourth night?

"Hey, wow, day four . . . I knew you could do it. Uh, hey, listen . . . I might not be around to send you a message tomorrow—"

Animatronics are banging at both doors. They're obviously getting agitated. They probably don't want you to make this recording.

"It's—It's been a bad night here." *Bang! Bang! Bang! Bang!* "For me. Umm . . . I—I'm kinda glad that I recorded my messages for you, er, when I did. H-hey, do me a favor—"

The banging gets louder and doesn't stop. You keep talking over it.

"Maybe sometime, eh, you could check inside those suits, in—in the back room? I'm gonna try to hold out . . . until someone . . . checks. Maybe it won't be so bad."

Will they do it? Will the next security guard return the favor and try to save *you*? Will it make a difference?

➤ TURN TO PAGE 187

➤ TURN TO PAGE 187

You want to hope this isn't the end, but having lived through almost five nights at Freddy's, you know the deal. Your replacement won't understand what you're saying, or they won't believe you, either, until it's too late.

Or maybe the animatronics won't even give them the opportunity to leave the Security Office. They're definitely more aggressive tonight, as if something has changed.

Maybe *you've* changed them, through your interactions with them this week. Some legacy.

"I—I—I always wondered what was in those empty heads . . . back there—"

A chime sounds behind you. What is that?

"You know . . ." You turn around, thinking Foxy has rebooted himself, but then you see what's behind him.

Freddy Fazbear. Something moans. Is it you?

"Oh no—"

The animatronics scream. All of them. The doors in the office pop open and the camera feeds cut out. The monitor spews static and snow dances across the screen.

The phone line goes dead.

. . .

. . .

When you come to (how?), it's dark. You can't move your head, but through two small eyeholes, you can just make out what appears to be the repair shop behind the stage.

I'm okay? you wonder.

Something smells bad. It might be you. *It's me.* Why can't you move your head, your hands?

I'm not okay.

All your choices have led you here, and now you're out of options. The only thing you can do is wait.

You can hardly believe it when the clock beside the security monitor clicks over to 6:00 a.m. You've survived your fifth and final night at Freddy's!

Now that the moment is finally here, you appreciate how much danger you were truly in. But by making all the right decisions along the way, you've survived one of the toughest challenges of your life.

You open the doors to the Security Office with a measure of apprehension, worrying even now that there's a twist or that someone is pulling a prank on you. The doors are pretty beat-up.

You walk slowly through Freddy Fazbear's Pizza, taking it all in for the last time. The place is a little messy, but that isn't your problem anymore.

"Not my circus, not my animatronics," you say.

You take a moment to look up at Freddy, Bonnie, and Chica on their stage. You can't help but feel bittersweet about leaving. Sure, they tried to kill you and they've given you nightmares for the rest of your life. But they probably have their reasons for it. They've clearly been through a lot themselves.

"No hard feelings."

You jump as the animatronics whir and run through their end-of-performance sequence, taking a bow. Saying good-bye.

You back up. "You are not supposed to be doing that."

Freddy turns his head to look at you. *It's time to go.*

➤ TURN TO PAGE 189

As you walk through the door and take your first steps into an uncertain future, you think you should feel lighter. You made it! You never have to come back here again. But something is still weighing on you. You feel like you might have some unfinished business here.

You don't like to leave a job undone, and deep inside you feel like you're abandoning your post. No one understands or cares about the animatronics more than you do. What will happen to them when you're not there to look after them?

What will they be able to get away with?

And you still don't have another job lined up. Even with Fazbear Entertainment's famously modest wage increases year after year, you still make more than minimum wage. What kind of work are you going to find out there? Coppelia is depending on you to keep a roof over her head and food on the table.

And to keep the monsters away, both real and imagined.

You wonder if you're truly done with these animatronics, and if they're truly done with you. You have the sense that Freddy, Bonnie, Chica, and Foxy can carry a grudge for a *long* time. But what could they hold against you?

"The worst thing I've done is *lived*," you say.

That might be enough.

You can think about it later. Right now, you can't wait to get home to your daughter. You're looking forward to getting a good night's sleep.

➤ TO START FROM THE BEGINNING, TURN TO PAGE 2

You scurry over to the vent opening and crouch to listen. You don't hear anything other than the murmur of air moving through the system. You don't really want to get much closer than that. You've seen enough movies to imagine a hand darting out of the vent to grab you and pull you inside.

Maybe just one quick peek, to be sure.

You lower yourself to the floor and start to stick your head inside, but suddenly Foxy the Pirate runs into the office, hook raised and a fierce expression on his face. He seems confused when he finds an empty chair. He looks around manically. He hasn't spotted you yet.

➤ IF YOU HAVE A <u>FLASHLIGHT</u>, YOU MAY USE IT ON PAGE 191
➤ IF YOU HAVE A <u>WATER PISTOL</u>, YOU MAY USE IT ON PAGE 176
➤ IF YOU TRY TO SNEAK INTO THE VENT, TURN TO PAGE 192

You grab your flashlight and jump to your feet to face Foxy. His head snaps in your direction and he bolts toward you. You switch on the flashlight and shine it in his face.

Foxy skids to a stop and shakes his head. He blinks a couple of times, and then raises an arm to shield his eyes.

Uh-oh.

He lowers the eyepatch over his right eye and squints his left a little, then rushes toward you.

Huh. You really thought that was going to work. Foxy always seemed a little twitchy about lights, and you thought all that time hiding in Pirate Cove would have made him more sensitive to disruption by the flashlight. But no, either he's learned to adapt or he is extremely intent on getting to you.

As he advances, you try moving the light around the room and the floor, hoping to distract him like a cat, but he only has an eye for you. Foxy reaches you in no time, backing you up against the lockers in the rear of the office, and his endoskeleton hand knocks the flashlight away.

Something grabs your left leg and squeezes hard enough to make the bones pop. You scream and look down to see a blue hand pulling on your ankle.

"Really?" you say. Foxy looks annoyed, too. He grabs your right arm and starts pulling you away from Bonnie. The tug-of-war continues as they fight over you like children trying to play with the same toy.

GAME OVER

➤ TO START FROM THE BEGINNING, TURN TO PAGE 2
➤ TO TRY THIS NIGHT AGAIN, TURN TO PAGE 158

Slowly, quietly, you back toward the vent, eyes locked on Foxy. He stalks the office, back and forth, back and forth. The two of you have that habit in common, only pacing helps you think, and you suppose, in his case, he needs an outlet for murderous rage. Maybe this is how he passes time in Pirate Cove behind that curtain.

Don't look at me, you think as you continue moving yourself inch by painstaking inch into the vent.

After all these years, you think about the animatronics as people, with personalities, thoughts, and desires. You have to remind yourself they're just machines. Metal skeletons wrapped in cloth and wire. Fancy puppets.

That *must* be all there is to them, because if they're actually intelligent beings, if they have *souls* . . . then no wonder they're so angry about being forced to perform for rowdy kids and harried parents, day in and day out. Anyone would want more. And they might be willing to do anything to get it.

One might even excuse them for their behavior. They didn't ask for any of this. It could be that it's Freddy, Bonnie, Chica, and Foxy who are the victims, in waking nightmares.

Walking nightmares.

Though you're in the shadows now inside the vent, Foxy finally spots you and is there in the blink of an eye. He embeds his hook in you.

"I'm sorry," you whisper.

GAME OVER

➤ TO START FROM THE BEGINNING, TURN TO PAGE 2
➤ TO TRY THIS NIGHT AGAIN, TURN TO PAGE 158

Trapped in the Security Office, you've never felt less safe at Freddy's than you do now. The animatronics are unusually aggressive and relentless. If they keep beating on those doors, it's only a matter of time before they give.

The only tool at your disposal is the phone on the desk. You pick up the handset and try to dial 9-1-1, but you can't get an outside line. You never did learn the access code that would allow you to call out.

But that doesn't mean you're completely helpless. You start dialing the extensions of other phones around the restaurant: the Dining Area, the Kitchen, Backstage. On the security cameras, you pick up the ringing, and immediately the banging ceases as the animatronics are lured away.

They'll be back. Probably soon. You hope if you keep this up, you can keep them busy chasing the ringing away from the office.

You notice the red light blinking on the phone. That wasn't there earlier, you're pretty sure. It could be an automated announcement from Management—they try to avoid direct conversations whenever possible. Or maybe someone has sent you a message.

You dial into the Voicemail system. It prompts you for a four-digit passcode.

➤ IF YOU TRY DIFFERENT COMBINATIONS, TURN TO PAGE 194
➤ IF YOU ENTER 1-9-8-3, TURN TO PAGE 195
➤ IF YOU ENTER 1-9-8-7, TURN TO PAGE 196
➤ IF YOU HAVE A TICKET, YOU MAY CHECK IT ON PAGE 197
➤ HANG UP AND WAIT OUT THE END OF YOUR SHIFT ON PAGE 188

You punch in the numbers 1-2-3-4 and the recorded voice says, "Incorrect passcode." You didn't expect it would be a combination an idiot would have on their luggage, but you never know.

Next you try 0-0-0-0, then 1-1-1-1, all the way through 9-9-9-9, but no dice. You might as well be rolling dice since there are 10,000 possible combinations, and the chances of you happening across the correct one before your shift ends are slim.

You shrug. It's not like you have anything better to do, and it's a fine way to kill time.

In frustration, you start typing numbers randomly. Amazingly, one of these attempts works. "Voicemail. You have one new message. Press 1 to play—"

Unfortunately, you were so engrossed in trying out different combinations, you forgot to continue calling around the restaurant. Something grabs you and pulls you backward, kicking and screaming, toward the vent. The phone handset clatters to the floor. A tinny voice comes out of the speaker, "You don't know me, but this is really important. Freddy and the others will . . ."

You'll never know who left the message or what was so important, but you're also not in much of a position to care anymore.

GAME OVER

➤ TO START FROM THE BEGINNING, TURN TO PAGE 2
➤ TO TRY THIS NIGHT AGAIN, TURN TO PAGE 158

Four digits . . . *Could be a year,* you think. You can't remember what year the first Freddy Fazbear's Pizza opened, or its predecessor, Fredbear's Family Diner, but one year does stick out. It was known as "the Big Bite" until it happened again four years later, kind of like how World War I was just "the Great War" until another one came along.

Speaking of tragedies that could have been avoided.

You punch in the numbers 1-9-8-3 and the phone line crackles. Then you hear . . . a sobbing child?

There's definitely a little boy crying on the other end of the line. He's shouting, "No! Let me go!"

You lean forward. "Hello? Hello? Are you there? Talk to me, kid!"

"No! Please, I don't want to!"

Your skin prickles. You realize you're listening to a recording. You can't help anyone.

". . . give you a closer look," another boy says, his voice mean and hard. You hear children's laughter and bubbly pop music, one of Fredbear's original hits, "The Secret Ingredient Is You," which you haven't heard in years.

"Hey, stop that! Put him down!" a man shouts. "Get back from the stage! Do *not* touch the bear."

People start shouting and screaming. The music plays on. The boy cries on.

Until—

Crunch.

You hang up the phone. But you can still hear a child crying. You twist around in your seat and see—

Crunch.

GAME OVER

➤ TO START FROM THE BEGINNING, TURN TO PAGE 2
➤ TO TRY THIS NIGHT AGAIN, TURN TO PAGE 158

Four digits . . . *Could be a year*, you think. You can't remember what year the first Freddy Fazbear's Pizza opened, or its predecessor, Fredbear's Family Diner, but one year does stick out. Who could forget the so-called "Bite of '87"?

You shudder. It's amazing that the human body can live without the frontal lobe.

You punch in the numbers 1-9-8-7 and there's a long pause before you hear two garbled words, slowed down: "Edocssap tcerrocni."

It takes you a moment to understand that it said "Incorrect passcode" in reverse. The Voicemail system is glitching out.

You try typing the numbers again. Or should you enter in 7-8-9-1 instead to get it back to normal? This time, you hear a series of clicks and the whir of a tape deck being rewound. Then a voice speaks.

It sounds familiar, then you recognize it as your own voice. You're listening to a recording you made some time ago for new employees. Someone has edited it.

"Hey, good job, night five! Um, hey, um, keep a close eye on things tonight, okay? Uh, we don't have a replacement for your shift yet, but we're working on it. Well, just get through one more night! Uh, hang in there! Good night!"

Thanks for the words of encouragement, past me. You wish you could leave a recording for that guy.

➤ KEEP DIALING TO THE END OF YOUR SHIFT AND TURN TO PAGE 188

You reach deep down into your pocket and fish out the prize ticket you found in Foxy's Pirate Cove. Now that you look at it in better light, you're not positive that those dark stains are from food at all.

You check the back of it, and just like you thought, there are four numbers written there in pen: 2, 0, 1, and 4.

"I wonder . . ." You punch them into the phone's keypad.

"Voicemail. You have one new message. Press 1 to play it, press 2 to listen to saved messages, press 3 to record a message for another extension."

You tap 1. "Message 1. Received five minutes ago." The line clicks and you hear a woman's voice, whispering.

"Ralph, if you're hearing this, you've probably realized by now that something is going on with the animatronics. They aren't acting normally, even for them—and it's because of you."

Who is this? How does she know my name? you think. *And how is any of this my fault?*

"You're probably wondering who I am. I bet you don't remember me, but you interviewed me for a summer job at Freddy's—and you decided not to hire me. Ralph, you saved my life."

➤ TURN TO PAGE 198

Management often invites you to screen applicants to see if they've got "the right stuff" for the job when there's more than one person interviewing. It isn't often that a woman wants to work here. So you do remember her now. Her name was Bronwen something. Only thing is, you gave her a glowing recommendation and were surprised when Management didn't hire her.

You might have been influenced because Bronwen reminded you of your daughter. She came across as smart, capable, and dependable— all the qualities you need to be a good security guard. She asked all the right questions, had all the right answers. If anything, she was too good for this place.

Maybe that's why they didn't hire her.

"My name is Bronwen Light. That summer I took a newspaper internship instead, and now I'm a reporter." She hesitates. "*Junior* reporter. I've been fascinated with Freddy's for years, though, and when we started hearing about . . . things . . . happening there, I made it my business to dig into the truth.

"I've found out so much, but my editor won't let me print any of it. I can't let it go. I just learned something, don't ask me how, that means you're in danger. We all are." She takes a deep breath. "Especially Coppelia."

Why does she know about your daughter? This is venturing into stalker territory. What's Bronwen's angle?

➤ TURN TO PAGE 199

"You have to trust me, Ralph. My sources say that the animatronics are planning something. That's right. They aren't just mindless puppets. You may not believe any of this.

"If you take a moment to think about it, you know it's true. They've been getting bored of night after night being the same, same, same. This whole week, they've been doing more and more than they used to—testing their limits, as well as yours. See, since you decided to leave, they started thinking about how *they* could leave, too."

That's impossible, you think.

"It's not impossible," she continues. "They've been messing with the power in the restaurant, redirecting it to their charging platforms. Storing up extra energy, so they can travel farther. One more night, and they'll be able to leave Freddy Fazbear's Pizza and terrorize people outside. And there'll be no stopping them.

"I know this is your last night on the job, but you have to come back tomorrow. You're the only one who can prevent them from escaping. If you can get under the stage, you can fix the charging platforms so they can't power up enough to leave.

"I bet you're wondering, *Well, why doesn't she do something?* I did. I tried. I broke into the restaurant a few nights ago. Jeremy got me. I mean, *Bonnie*. Sorry about that mess."

➤ TURN TO PAGE 200

"I've held on as long as I can, but I can't make it any longer." She laughs, bitterly. "So this is my last night, too. Don't worry about trying to save me. It's too late. Just worry about saving your daughter. Save everyone else. Please, Ralph.

"If you find my phone in the restaurant, do me a favor. Call my mother, let her know what happened to me. She'll know what to do, and if we're lucky, she'll find my research and the stories I've written, and we'll be able to make sure that Fazbear Entertainment never— Oh."

You hear a child's laughter and then a monstrous, mechanical roar.

The line crackles and you hear strange tones and noise. Then Bronwen speaks again, but her voice is garbled and low: "It's me."

Click.

"End of message."

You sit for a moment in silence, watching the clock tick over to 6:00 a.m. When you try to play Bronwen's message again, it's gone, as if it had never happened.

You could have hallucinated it, you think. That would be the easy way out. You survived your fifth and final night at Freddy's. You never have to come back here again. You get to leave and go home to your daughter and put this place behind you.

Bronwen was practically a stranger; you don't owe her anything. But she chose to run to danger, to give up her life to protect other people.

You were right about her.

You sigh. "It's not over."

➤ TURN TO PAGE 241

Night 6—12:00 a.m.

Management approved your request for overtime without asking any questions. They let you know they're still looking for your replacement, as there haven't been any responses to their advertisement yet. "We'll see how it goes tonight," you told them.

If you fail tonight, they won't need a night watchman, and they'll have a much bigger problem on their hands.

If you succeed, Management won't be so enthusiastic about welcoming you back.

You check the cameras like you always do. Freddy, Bonnie, Chica, and Foxy are where they're supposed to be, and they're staying put. That alone seems suspicious, especially after they were so active last night.

Maybe they're tired. You laugh.

If you believe Bronwen Light, the animatronics are storing up all the power they can before they leave the restaurant. In that case, you should head out now while they're dormant.

You've already consulted with your friend Dave in Maintenance: You can't just switch off the power from the Breaker Room this time because the charging platforms are on their own power supply with a backup generator. So you have to find some way to disrupt them.

The fastest way to the stage is through the West Hall. But if the animatronics realize what you're doing, the *safest* way is through the vents.

➤ IF YOU GET INTO THE VENTILATION SHAFT, TURN TO PAGE 202
➤ IF YOU TAKE THE DIRECT ROUTE TO THE DINING AREA, TURN TO PAGE 203
➤ IF YOU WATCH THE CAMERAS AND WAIT A WHILE, TURN TO PAGE 204

"Better safe than sorry," you say as you crawl into the Security Office vent. Somewhere along the way, these narrow passageways became less frightening. At least you only need to watch in two directions for anyone attacking you, forward and behind, and you can tell if an animatronic is in the vents with you.

Unfortunately, something smells terrible inside. Probably a dead rat. There are poison traps hidden all over the restaurant, but the critters still crawl into the walls and vents to die. You cover your nose and press on.

You know your way around these corridors now, so it's no problem getting to the Dining Area. Before you pop out, you take a quick peek—and you see two big, blue rabbit feet right in front of the vent opening.

Is Bonnie standing watch? It looks like Freddy and Chica have wandered off as well. If you can fix the charging platforms on the stage, you'll have to lure them back somehow.

You swallow. That won't be easy.

It also won't be easy getting to the stage with Bonnie in the way. You either have to find a way around him or a way to distract him.

➤ IF YOU WAIT FOR BONNIE TO LEAVE, TURN TO PAGE 205
➤ IF YOU GO BACKSTAGE TO CAUSE A DISTRACTION, TURN TO PAGE 206
➤ IF YOU TRY CRAWLING TO THE OTHER SIDE OF THE DINING AREA, TURN TO PAGE 217

You turn on the lights in the West Hall to check for Bonnie before you peer out the door, but the way looks clear. You even check the Supply Closet camera to be extra sure, though all the animatronics are still on the stage. Then you walk cautiously down the West Hall toward the Dining Area, stopping and listening every few feet.

Nothing.

Your experiences this week have conditioned you to fear the worst, to jump at every sound and shadow. By the time you get to the Dining Area and see Freddy, Bonnie, and Chica in their usual positions, with no signs of movement, you're starting to feel a little silly about it all.

"Well, let's get this over with," you say. Your voice echoes in the empty space. You watch the animatronics, but they don't react to your presence at all.

It's hard to believe they could be "planning" to escape the restaurant. Where would they go? What's their goal?

You walk around the stage to the access panel near the back. This is where the staff selects the songs the trio performs. The lights, sound, and choreography are programmed for each of their thirty-something musical numbers, but there are manual overrides in case something happens. You should be able to use it to manage their power usage.

There's also a hatch beside the panel that opens into the crawlspace under the stage.

➤ IF YOU CLIMB INTO THE CRAWLSPACE, TURN TO PAGE 219
➤ IF YOU OPEN THE ACCESS PANEL, TURN TO PAGE 222

You decide to wait a little longer and watch the animatronics before you sabotage the restaurant. Bronwen might have been telling the truth, but her suspicions could be wrong.

You alternate between the cameras for the Show Stage and Pirate Cove. After two hours, none of the animatronics have so much as moved. You guess this is what the job would be like if the animatronics *didn't* roam around at night.

It's kind of boring.

You're again starting to think that perhaps you imagined everything this week. The best evidence that Freddy, Bonnie, Chica, and Foxy didn't really try to kill you is the fact that you're still here. What chance would you have against all four of them? You're just one person, without a weapon.

If the animatronics aren't a threat tonight, then you should keep an eye out for intruders. You click through the other cameras, but everything is quiet. The way it's supposed to be.

You yawn. You click back to the Show Stage—and suddenly you're wide-awake.

Freddy's gone!

Where did he go, though? You didn't see him on any of the cameras just now. You cycle through them again. No sign of Freddy. You listen. You can't hear his creepy music, either.

You click back on the Show Stage. Now Bonnie's gone!

Oh no.

They aren't coming after you, which means . . . they've left. You're too late.

GAME OVER

➤ TO START FROM THE BEGINNING, TURN TO PAGE 2
➤ TO TRY THIS NIGHT AGAIN, TURN TO PAGE 201

By 3:00 a.m., you have to accept the fact that Bonnie is not budging. He must know you're in the vent, but he doesn't seem interested in coming after you.

He's distracting me, you think. *So the others can leave.*

You may already be too late to stop them. Then you hear the phone ring back in the Security Office. No one ever calls you here. No one ever calls anyone in the middle of the night unless there's an emergency.

It will take you too long to crawl through the vents back to the Security Office, so you decide to test your theory. You slip out of the vent. Bonnie watches you, but he doesn't move.

Is he broken?

But no, his eyelids blink, and his mouth . . . He's smiling. A shiver runs down your spine.

Then you turn and run to the Security Office. The phone continues ringing, and a child's laugh follows you from the Dining Area.

You dash into the office and answer the phone. "Hello?"

"Hi, Daddy." It's Coppelia.

"Pel! Honey, what's wrong?"

"Nothing! Your friends came over and woke me up."

"Someone's there?"

The phone gets muffled as she covers the handset. "You want to talk to him?" she says.

You squeeze the handset as she hands the phone to someone. "Who is this?" you whisper. The connection crackles.

"*It's me.*" Freddy Fazbear laughs and hangs up.

GAME OVER

➤ TO START FROM THE BEGINNING, TURN TO PAGE 2
➤ TO TRY THIS NIGHT AGAIN, TURN TO PAGE 201

You leave Bonnie behind and make your way through the vents to the Backstage opening. The stench is coming from the small room. It's strong enough to make you gag as you crawl out of the shaft.

What died in here?

You look around, feeling unsettled. You know what you're looking for. That empty Freddy suit you saw earlier.

It's in a different position from what you remembered, now hunched over in the corner of the room next to some storage shelves. Someone has attached a spare Freddy head, one of the earlier models from the Fredbear days, only twisted around backward so it's facing the wall. The air is thick with flies swarming around it, crawling over it. Something is in its right hand.

Every fiber of your being is screaming for you to look away, get away from here, but you have to see. You are standing right in front of the costume now, close enough to recognize the object in its hand as a large mobile phone.

"I'm so sorry," you whisper.

➤ IF YOU TAKE THE <u>PHONE</u>, TURN TO PAGE 207
➤ IF YOU REMOVE THE <u>HEAD</u> TO LOOK INSIDE, TURN TO PAGE 227

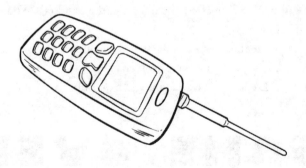

You take the mobile phone, saying a silent "thank-you" and wipe it off on your pants. You scroll through the contacts. There are some entries named in codes like "Deep Dish," and others are labeled "Backstage," "Dining Area," and "Restrooms." She's entered the numbers for every phone in the restaurant and home numbers for many of the employees. The last one she dialed is "Security Office."

Heavy footsteps approach the door to the room you're in. You see a shadow under the door.

You needed a distraction, and now you've got one. You press ENTER and dial the Security Office. Far off, you hear the phone ring.

The shadow disappears and the footsteps hurry away. You keep the line ringing and stand up. You place a hand on the Freddy head and say, "I'll finish this."

➤ ADD THE MOBILE PHONE <u>BONUS ITEM</u> TO YOUR INVENTORY AND HEAD
TO THE STAGE ON PAGE 210

Hoping to overload the animatronics, you flip all six switches to the "up" position. The switchbox hums and gets warm to the touch, and blue electricity arcs from the cables to every metal surface in the crawl-space. From below, the charging platform sparks and buzzes dangerously.

You clamber out of the crawlspace and slam the hatch shut. The lights in the Dining Area flicker. You may not have much time before you blow every fuse in the place. How are you going to get the animatronics back up on that stage?

➤ IF YOU GET UP ON THE STAGE AND MAKE SOME NOISE, TURN TO PAGE 211
➤ IF YOU GO TO THE ACCESS PANEL AND START UP A SHOW, TURN TO PAGE 212

Everyone knows the best way to fix a technical problem is to reverse the polarity. You confidently flip all six switches to the "down" position. The room suddenly becomes very quiet as the power cuts out.

You hear a mechanical *kerchunk* and red lights come on. The system has switched over to backup power, but the animatronics have already drained the battery almost all the way. By reversing the flow, you hope that getting them back on their charging plates will *draw* the power from their batteries into the backup battery.

You slip out of the crawlspace and lower the hatch. The lights are even dimmer than before. Now how are you going to get the animatronics back up on that stage?

➤ IF YOU GET UP THERE AND MAKE SOME NOISE, TURN TO PAGE 211
➤ IF YOU GO TO THE ACCESS PANEL AND START UP A SHOW,
   TURN TO PAGE 220

With the Dining Area clear, you head straight to the stage. Bronwen said you needed to get under it to fix the charging platform. You get to the hatch for the crawlspace and climb inside, closing it over your head.

Thick power cables snake out of the switchbox for the charging platform, more than there should be. And they probably shouldn't be sparking like that. There are also six small metal switches, alternating in the "up" and "down" positions.

Bronwen didn't tell you how to fix the charging platforms, but you find a scrap of paper crumpled on the floor. It's a diagram of the correct positions for each switch, which seems to have been torn off and discarded. The first three switches are supposed to be up, the next two are down, and the sixth in neutral.

You restore all the switches to their original settings, but of course nothing happens. This isn't going to stop the animatronics—they're already powered up, so you need to short them out or drain their batteries back to normal.

➤ IF YOU FLIP ALL THE SWITCHES UP, TURN TO PAGE 208
➤ IF YOU FLIP ALL THE SWITCHES DOWN, TURN TO PAGE 209

You climb up to the stage and look out at the empty Dining Area. You picture it filled to capacity with kids and parents, like it was in the good old days. Then you blink, and everyone is dead, the tablecloths and floor slick with blood. You rub your eyes and shake your head. When you look up again, everything is back to normal.

"I have a bad feeling about this," you say. Then you start clapping and whooping and shouting at the top of your lungs.

"Come and get me!" you call out. "Bonnie! Chica! Freddy!"

But they don't come. Maybe they see through your ruse, or they've already left the building.

You laugh. After all this time, a week of sneaking around, making as little noise as possible, the moment you become an easy target, they're nowhere to be found.

You sit on the edge of the stage, kicking your legs against it. It's almost 6:00 a.m. You survived yet another night. You're going to go home and grab Coppelia and get out of town. As far as you can go, farther than the animatronics can travel, even if they manage to recharge.

A shadow moves, slipping from the Pirate Cove. You forgot about Foxy.

But he didn't forget about you.

GAME OVER

➤ TO START FROM THE BEGINNING, TURN TO PAGE 2
➤ TO TRY THIS NIGHT AGAIN, TURN TO PAGE 201

You hurry over to the access panel and open it. Inside is a small green LCD screen, a number pad, and a silver lock with a silver key already inside.

"That's a security issue." You turn the key and the stage lights come up, brighter than usual because of all the juice flowing into them. Energy crackles along the charging pads, but you hope the animatronics don't notice.

There's supposed to be a manual with a list of codes for songs and other commands, but you don't know where it is. So you punch in some random numbers until music starts playing.

It's an upbeat number with lots of bass. That should make Bonnie happy. The phrase "44—POWR UP YOR L1FE" appears on the display. One of your favorites!

The recorded announcer introduces the animatronics on the stage—and they come! Unable to resist their programming, Freddy, Bonnie, and Chica take their places. As soon as they step onto their charging platforms, their limbs go rigid and they start shaking and smoking. Their eyes light up and explode, showering the stage with sparks.

They scream.

Then the lights go out and fall silent. The animatronics slump, heads down, arms slack, puppets with their strings cut. Their fur is scorched and the smoky Dining Area smells like burned barbecue.

Sadness washes over you. Freddy, Bonnie, and Chica are dead. You succeeded in stopping them, but you failed your promise to protect them.

➤ GO HOME ON PAGE 213

It's still only 4:00 a.m., but you don't see any point in sticking around Freddy Fazbear's Pizza, and you can't wait to get home to see your daughter.

When you get there, all the lights are on in your house, and Coppelia is waiting for you on the couch in the living room.

"Hey. What are you doing up, kiddo?" You sit next to her and sink into the cushions. You didn't realize how tired you are and how much your body aches until now. You feel like you haven't stopped moving all night—all week. You've been running on adrenaline so long, it's a miracle your body hasn't completely shut down already.

"I had a nightmare," Coppelia says.

You chuckle. "Yeah, me too. Three of them."

"But it's over now," she says.

"Yeah." Wait. "Did I say three nightmares? I meant four."

"What's wrong, Daddy?" she asks.

"I forgot about something . . . at work." What is Foxy going to do there, all on his own now? They're going to shut down the restaurant, this time for good. You're sure of it. That poor old pirate.

Someone knocks on the door. Coppelia stands up. "Who could that be?"

One of the best things about your job was that work never followed you home. Until now.

"Don't go near the door!" you shout as the knocks turn into slashes that reduce the door to splinters. Foxy breaks in.

➤ TURN TO PAGE 228

Coppelia raises her left hand and aims a gun at Foxy. You do a double take, wondering where she got it from. Then you realize it's the water pistol you gave her the other night, painted black.

"'Try holy water, death breath!'" She pumps the trigger and water shoots out of the tip. It splashes all over Foxy's chest. Some of it gets inside through the tears in his costume. Something pops and sparks fly out. His eyes dim and he topples forward.

"Whoa," you say. "You're a natural. But where'd you get holy water from?"

She rolls her eyes. "It's a line from, like, my favorite movie ever."

It's only when you hug that you feel how shaken up she is.

The next morning, a representative from Fazbear Entertainment comes to collect Foxy. She hands you a bill for more than you earn in a year: the cost of repairing the animatronics they say you broke.

"What about the people we saved?" you ask.

"That never happened. And if you say it did, you'll go to jail." She smiles. "You could always come back to work, with a new contract and a portion of your debt deducted from each paycheck."

Absolutely not, you think. "I'll consider it," you say. You have your principles, and you're honestly afraid to ever return there, but you owe them a *lot* of money.

GAME OVER

➤ TO START FROM THE BEGINNING, TURN TO PAGE 2
➤ TO TRY THIS NIGHT AGAIN, TURN TO PAGE 201

Coppelia raises her left hand and brandishes a ballpoint pen.

"I know they say the pen is mightier than the sword," you say, "but they never defended themselves against a three-hundred-pound animatronic fox possessed by the vengeful spirit of a murdered child."

She twists the pen and pulls off one end of it to reveal a flathead screwdriver. That's one of the Freddy Fazbear Pizza's Employee of the Month rewards!

She doesn't wait for Foxy to attack. She lunges at him and jabs the pen into his left eye, the one not covered by an eyepatch—temporarily blinding him.

You both flee the house and get into your car, driving north as far as you can go. Coppelia uses the mobile phone to call the police to warn them about an animatronic on the loose, but they don't believe her and suggest you both come in to file a report in person. She hangs up.

You eye the rearview mirrors, fearing you'll see Foxy chasing after you.

"We'll be all right," you say. "He has to run out of power sometime. But there's one more person we should call. Can you dial Mom?"

"You want me to call Mom?" Coppelia fiddles with the phone.

"Not *your* mother, Bronwen Light's. We owe her our lives, and her mom deserves to know what happened to her."

GAME OVER

➤ TO START FROM THE BEGINNING, TURN TO PAGE 2
➤ TO TRY THIS NIGHT AGAIN, TURN TO PAGE 201

"You make an excellent point," she says. "I've got nothing."

Foxy rushes toward her but you tackle him to the floor while Coppelia watches in horror.

When Foxy begins eviscerating you with his hook, she screams and picks up the phone. She weighs it, looking from the phone to Foxy.

"Run," you gurgle.

She takes the phone and runs with it into her bedroom.

You hear her calling for the police, and then you black out.

When you regain consciousness, the door of Coppelia's bedroom has been destroyed.

"Pel!" You cough. You're cold and can't stand, probably because most of your blood has seeped into the ugly carpeting beneath you. You grab the phone cord and pull it back to you, but it's no longer attached to the phone. The end of it is roughly cut, like sharp teeth bit through it.

You lie on the floor, listening to sirens that never arrive and rewinding all your choices, trying different ones, hoping for a better outcome.

You don't mind sacrificing yourself for your daughter, you only wish you knew she'd be all right without you.

As you slip away, you dream that Foxy returns to your home with Chica. Chica looks different without her bib. She leans over you, and in your daughter's voice she whispers, "It's me."

GAME OVER

➤ TO START FROM THE BEGINNING, TURN TO PAGE 2
➤ TO TRY THIS NIGHT AGAIN, TURN TO PAGE 201

You decide to go around Bonnie to the other side of the Dining Area, and sneak to the stage from there.

You thought you knew your way around these vents, but you get impossibly lost after a few minutes.

I should be there by now, you think. *It's like they've moved around since the other night.*

You crawl around for almost an hour without getting any closer to the stage or finding any openings you can exit from. You're drenched in sweat and grime, and dead bugs and webs cling to your skin. It stinks and you can't breathe; you swear that the corridors are getting narrower.

Then you hear metal rattling and the thumping of someone else in the vents, closing in on you quickly. Bonnie? Foxy? Who cares—you have to get out of there!

➤ TURN TO PAGE 225

You drag yourself out of the ventilation shaft and lie on the floor, trying to catch your breath. You're so exhausted, you can't even open your eyes or lift your head. From the smell of cleaning chemicals and the feel of the cool tiles under your cheek, you realize you're in one of the Restrooms.

A groaning voice echoes around you. Someone is standing right over you. You crack open an eye and see a large chicken foot inches from your face.

Before you can react, Chica raises her foot and stomps on your head. Your skull cracks open like an egg.

GAME OVER

➤ TO START FROM THE BEGINNING, TURN TO PAGE 2
➤ TO TRY THIS NIGHT AGAIN, TURN TO PAGE 201

Bronwen had said you need to get *under the stage*. You have to trust that she knows something you don't—that's why you're here in the first place.

You crouch in front of the corrugated metal hatch in the floor and place your fingertips on it. You feel a slight vibration and heavy footsteps, moving fast.

Alarmed, you glance up at the stage, but the animatronics are still there. Then what—

The answer comes to you even before you turn and see him barreling toward you. Foxy.

Bronwen didn't mention him, and of course *his* charging platform is over in Pirate Cove. He's in even rougher shape than usual after last night's attempts to kill you, and you suspect that he isn't part of tonight's escape plan. He might be feeling bitter about that. He might want to take revenge on you.

Or maybe he just wants to help the other animatronics realize their hopes and dreams.

There's nowhere to run, so in a desperate attempt to stop Foxy, you yank open the access panel and turn the key inside to switch on the animatronics. You stab the song select button a couple of times to choose a performance.

But all that happens is Freddy, Bonnie, and Chica turn their heads to observe what Foxy does to you.

GAME OVER

➤ TO START FROM THE BEGINNING, TURN TO PAGE 2
➤ TO TRY THIS NIGHT AGAIN, TURN TO PAGE 201

You open the access panel beside the stage. Inside is a small green LCD screen, a number pad, and a silver lock with a silver key already inside.

"Here goes nothing." You turn the key and the stage lights come up at half brightness. You jump when the light illuminates a shadow figure behind the stage. It looks like Freddy Fazbear, but his fur is lighter, more golden, and he has no eyes. Even so, you know he is looking at you.

You also know that if you look away from him, you will be lost. You feel for the keypad and blindly punch a bunch of numbers to call up a song.

You recognize it at once: It's "Everyone Needs Some Downtime," a slow song that is usually played when kids are extra hyped up at a party, and just before the restaurant closes for the night.

The Golden Freddy giggles like a mischievous child and keeps staring. You train your eyes on him, forcing yourself not to blink.

The recorded announcer starts introducing the animatronics on the stage. Time passes and you think they aren't going to come, until you hear their heavy footsteps approach and climb the steps to the stage. You want to watch to make sure they return to their positions, but you dare not look away from Golden Freddy.

Can the others see him? you wonder. They're completely ignoring you.

Maybe because they figure I'm already dead.

>TURN TO PAGE 221

Freddy starts singing, Bonnie rocks his guitar, and Chica struts her stuff. You aren't sure it's working, but as the song wears on—and it's one of the longest in the catalog at seven minutes and forty-eight seconds—they slow down, slurring their words, and getting clumsy.

Go home, you're drunk, you think, at the same time another, forceful thought intrudes with *It's me.*

You *see* the words in your head. You hear them and you feel them. They *hurt*.

You wince and stagger under the weight of Golden Freddy's mind. Blood trickles from your right nostril. You taste it, salty and metallic, on your lips.

The song ends and the animatronics fall silent and still. You risk a quick glance to the stage. Their eyes are closed. They're sleeping.

You take a deep breath. It worked.

You turn back toward Golden Freddy and he suddenly appears in front of your face, mouth open and screaming.

You stagger and fall to your knees. Golden Freddy puts his hands on either side of your head.

➤ TURN TO PAGE 226

You should be able to tell whether anything is wrong with the charging platforms by checking the access panel. If something is amiss that can't be adjusted from the manual controls, you'll crawl under the stage like Bronwen suggested.

As soon as you flip open the door on the access panel, Freddy Fazbear's head whips in your direction. You're so surprised, you yelp and backpedal away from the stage.

Freddy's eyes glow as he stares down at you. He steps to the edge and hops down to the floor. *Thud.* He walks toward you while the speakers play classical music.

You know you should run. You want to run. But you are rooted to the spot, waiting for him to reach you.

Bronwen was right, you think. Even if you could move, where could you go to get away from him and the others? The restaurant can no longer contain them.

Freddy is close now. He opens his mouth. You wince, expecting him to scream, but instead he laughs. It sounds like a child's laughter. More children laugh—Bonnie and Chica are watching you from the stage, mouths opening and closing.

"You're just kids?" you say. "Who?"

Freddy's face is inches from your head. He leans down. You wonder what it will be like living without your frontal lobe.

A warped, garbled voice says, *"It's me."*

GAME OVER

➤ TO START FROM THE BEGINNING, TURN TO PAGE 2
➤ TO TRY THIS NIGHT AGAIN, TURN TO PAGE 201

You keep going, deeper and deeper into the ventilation shaft. You take a turn, and the air is still and stale and smells like death. You're not even certain you're in the main restaurant anymore. You think you might be in the abandoned expansion, which you expect will never be completed now. There should be an exit here somewhere.

Occasionally, you can hear the animatronic knocking around in the shaft behind you, but you've put some distance between you. Now you can feel them more than hear them, in the vibrations of the metal, and the aura of malevolence that permeates their presence.

You see an opening far ahead. It might be the same one you passed earlier.

➤ EXIT THE VENTILATION SHAFT ON PAGE 218
➤ KEEP CRAWLING ON PAGE 224

"You are in a maze of twisty little corridors, all alike," you mutter, just to hear something. Your voice echoes up and down the ventilation shaft. "You are likely to be eaten by Foxy."

You stop for a moment to rest. You don't hear the animatronic anymore, but it's completely dark in here and you can't hear any of the sounds of the restaurant. You don't know what time it is—it could be morning already.

"Freddy has left the building." You giggle. You are probably going mad. What are you doing here? You had something to do, but you're already having trouble remembering.

"It was my last week before retirement," you say bitterly. "I was out. But they pulled me back in."

The stage! You have to get to the stage.

You sigh and continue crawling, though you barely have the strength to go on. There's that opening again! Is it the same one?

➤ EXIT THE VENTILATION SHAFT ON PAGE 218
➤ KEEP CRAWLING ON PAGE 225
➤ IF YOU HAVE THE BONUS ITEM AND WANT TO USE IT, YOU MAY DO SO ON PAGE 242

Your knees and elbows throb from crawling, but you crawl like you've never crawled before. You take one turn after another, trying to lose your pursuer, but they only get closer and closer.

You see an opening ahead.

➤ **EXIT THE VENTILATION SHAFT ON PAGE 218**
➤ **KEEP CRAWLING ON PAGE 223**

Itsmeitsmeitsmeitsmeitsmeitsmeitsmeitsmeitsmeitsmeitsme
itsmeitsmeitsmeitsmeitsmeitsmeitsmeitsmeitsmeitsmeitsme
itsmeitsmeitsmeitsmeitsmeitsmeitsmeitsmeitsmeitsmeitsme
itsmeitsmeitsmeitsmeitsmeitsmeitsmeitsmeitsmeitsmeitsme
itsmeitsmeitsmeitsmeitsmeitsmeitsmeitsmeitsmeitsmeitsme
itsmeitsmeitsmeitsmeitsmeitsme

Just under the angry onslaught of noise, you hear a soft voice, a warm and gentle one. A woman saying, "It's me. Thank you . . . You did it. She'll be all right now. She's safe. She's safe . . ."

Itsmeitsmeitsmeitsmeitsmeitsmeitsmeitsmeitsmeitsme
itsmeshessafeitsmeitsmeitsmeitsmeshessafeitsmeitsmeitsme
itsmeitsmeitsmeitsmeitsmeitsmeitsmeitsmeitsmeitsme
itsmeshessafeshessafeshessafeitsmeitsmeitsmeitsmeitsme
itsmeitsmeitsmeitsmeitsmeitsmeitsmeitsmeshessafeshessafe
shessafeshessafeitsmeshessafeshessafeshessafeitsmeshessafeshessafeshes
safeitsmeitsmeitsmeitsmeitsmeitsmeitsmeitsmeitsmeitsme
shessafeshessafeshessafeshessafeshessafeshessafeshessafeshessafeshes
safeshessafeshessafeshessa feshessafeshessafeshessafeshessafeshessafe

She's safe. You smile and go to sleep.

⁜⁜⁜⁜THE END⁜⁜⁜⁜

> ⮞ NOW THAT YOU HAVE THE MOBILE PHONE <u>BONUS ITEM</u>, EMPTY YOUR INVENTORY OF EVERYTHING BUT THE PHONE, THEN TURN TO PAGE 2 AND START OVER FOR A BRAND-NEW ADVENTURE

With trembling fingers, you try to remove the head, but it's stuck fast. Flies swarm around you, buzzing and brushing against your face and hands. You squint your eyes and hold your breath against the putrid scent of rot.

You try twisting the head from side to side, and it starts to give. You gradually work it all the way around, and something dark and thick oozes from the neck seam. You peer through the dark eye holes and get a glimpse of what's inside. You see a body with a nametag: Bronwen. Or what's left of her.

You turn and vomit. When you look up through the tears and flies, you find Bonnie standing over you, holding another Bonnie head.

He wants to return your favor of reattaching his head, only he has to remove your old one first.

GAME OVER

➤ TO START FROM THE BEGINNING, TURN TO PAGE 2
➤ TO TRY THIS NIGHT AGAIN, TURN TO PAGE 201

You jump up and move yourself between Foxy and Coppelia. Foxy points his hook at you and screams.

"Leave her alone!" you shout back at him. You cast your eyes around your house for something you can use to fight back and protect your daughter.

"What the heck? Is that Foxy the Pirate?" your daughter says.

"Who taught you to talk like that?" you say.

"Really? Is this the time to be a dad?" Coppelia stands beside you.

"I'll distract him while you sneak out the back," you whisper.

She shakes her head. "I'm not going without you. We can take him."

"With what?"

➤ IF YOU GAVE COPPELIA A <u>WATER PISTOL</u>, TURN TO PAGE 214

➤ IF YOU GAVE HER A <u>BALLPOINT PEN</u>, TURN TO PAGE 215

➤ IF YOU GAVE HER A DIFFERENT ITEM OR NOTHING, TURN TO PAGE 216

When you get home at 6:30 a.m., you wish you could go to bed, but your day isn't over just yet. Now it's time for your second, but most important job: parenting. This one is full-time and pays nil, but you wouldn't have it any other way. However, getting your eleven-year-old daughter, Coppelia, up and ready for school is more challenging than anything Freddy Fazbear's Pizza could throw your way.

You peek into her bedroom and see her still snoozing peacefully. Books are scattered across her bedspread and on the floor, and an open one lies on her chest, rising and falling with her steady breathing. She was clearly up late last night, reading, as usual.

You laugh a little when you see drool in the corner of her mouth and a damp spot on her pillowcase. *I wish I had a camera*, you think. So you study her a little longer, trying to hold on to this memory for later.

You go into the kitchen to make breakfast, intentionally banging pots and pans around as you cook eggs and bacon. You can't help but think of Chica, and you force the thought away. You're off the clock now, and you will not let the animatronics live rent-free in your head.

➤ TURN TO PAGE 230

The combination of Coppelia's alarm clock and the aroma of bacon is enough to wake her. She pads out into the kitchen in her rocket ship pajamas, hair a tangled mess, and her face lights up when she sees you.

"Missed me, huh?" you say, twirling your spatula.

"No, I just love bacon. So much." She gives you a hug. "And by extension, the person making it for me."

You laugh.

"But seriously, I missed you," she says.

"While you were sleeping?"

"Especially then. I never sleep well when you aren't home."

"I hate leaving you. But it's just for this week."

She sees the concern on your face and puts a hand over her mouth. "Oh, Dad. I didn't mean to guilt-trip you. I'm fine, really. Mrs. Andrews always looks in on me, and she hears everything that goes on around here."

"That's an understatement." You smile. You're grateful to have someone close by to watch the house when you're away, but you've never worried that Coppelia will get into any trouble on her own. If anything, she's keeping an eye on kindly Mrs. Andrews, who had sadly lost her own daughter at a young age years ago, and has been overprotective of the neighborhood kids since.

Coppelia reaches for the tray of cooked bacon.

You slap her hand away. "You are not getting one slice of bacon until you're dressed for school."

She sticks her tongue out and disappears into her room.

➤ TURN TO PAGE 231

Coppelia comes back in record time with her hair neatly tied in a ponytail, a bedazzled purple T-shirt, tights, and a jean jacket. She sits down, and you put a heaping amount of bacon on her plate that she immediately starts shoveling into her mouth.

"How was work?" she asks.

"Uneventful," you lie.

"Sounds like my dream job," she says. "Sitting at a desk in the middle of the night. Pushing buttons. I would catch up on so much reading. Until boredom kills me."

"You would not be killed by boredom at Freddy's," you say. "And promise me you'll never work there."

She laughs. "Okay . . . Sure."

"Now how was *your* day?"

You catch up with each other while you eat breakfast. Then she notices the time on the Kit-Cat Klock and jumps up. "My bus!"

She shoves another piece of bacon in her mouth and grabs her backpack by the kitchen door. She rummages around in it. "Crud! Do you have a pen? I have to finish my homework on the bus."

You raise an eyebrow. "Why didn't you do it last night?"

"Because I couldn't find my pen. Keep up, Dad."

➤ IF YOU HAVE THE BALLPOINT PEN AND GIVE IT TO HER, REMOVE IT FROM YOUR INVENTORY AND TURN TO PAGE 232

➤ TELL HER TO BORROW A PEN, AND TURN TO PAGE 52

You grab the pen from your pocket. "Here you go. Don't lose this one." You toss it to her.

She catches it expertly. She should really be on a sports team, but all she wants to do is read, tinker with projects in the basement, and play the Sega Genesis.

She's a great kid, you think. *I don't know how I got so lucky.*

"Thanks." She looks at the pen. "'Freddy Fazbear's Pizza Employee of the Month.' Don't you have like a drawer full of these? You're the best worker there. Not that the bar is that high."

"Hey! Give me my pen back."

"Nope!" She twists the pen and discovers there's a screwdriver inside. "Wicked."

"Yeah . . . You probably shouldn't be bringing that to school." You stand up. "I'll find you another pen."

The bus honks outside.

"Too late! Gotta go!" She runs to the door.

A moment later, she runs back and gives you a kiss on the cheek. "Love you!"

And then she's gone, with your pen in hand.

You already miss her. At least working the night shift doesn't take away your time together, though you don't like the idea of leaving her home alone, even under the sometimes too watchful eyes of the neighbors.

Just four more days. You yawn and head to bed.

➤ TURN TO PAGE 52

As soon as you get home, you rush to your daughter's room and check on her. She's sleeping with her left leg sticking out from under the covers and a pillow over her face.

You must have spaced out for a minute because the next thing you know, she screams and throws the pillow at your head. You catch it and hold it to your chest.

"What? What's wrong?" you say.

"Why were you standing there staring at me?" she says.

"I was about to wake you for school . . . I'm sorry. It's been a weird night."

She pushes her hair back from her face. "It's okay. It was just kind of creepy. When I first woke up, I must have been still dreaming. You looked like that Fredbear thing from your job."

"You mean Freddy Fazbear?"

"Whatever. He weirds me out. They all do."

She's never gotten over the time you brought her to work to meet the animatronics when she was seven, and they made her cry so hard she threw up her pizza and cake. She had nightmares for at least a week afterward.

"Never mind. It's just me, your loving Dadbear!" You open your arms for a hug.

She squints at you. "Please never say 'Dadbear' again."

You feel bad about scaring her and ruining her morning. You don't want her to have bad memories of you like that. Gifts always make her feel better.

➤ IF YOU GIVE HER THE COIN, TURN TO PAGE 234
➤ IF YOU KEEP THE COIN, TURN TO PAGE 86

"Oh, hey, I got you something." You flip the plastic coin over to her.

The coin falls on her superheroes bedspread and she grabs it. She holds it up and closes one eye to inspect it with the other.

"I just said that your freaky robot friends freak me out. And this one is the freakiest of all."

"Foxy was always my favorite."

She looks at you. "That explains a lot about you."

"I wasn't expecting this kind of attitude until you were a teenager."

"I'm almost," she says.

"You're not, and don't be in a rush to grow up. Anyway, that is a collectible gold treasure coin."

She bites down on it. "It's fake."

You grimace. "Uh, it was kind of dirty . . ."

"It's all scratched up and mangled."

"Fine." You hold out your hand. "Give it back."

She flips it in the air and catches it. "I love it. Because you gave it to me."

You smile.

"Even if it's just some junk you found on the floor at work or something. It's nice to know you were thinking of me."

You sigh. "Always, kiddo. I'll go make breakfast while you change for school."

"If I get heads, you have to make pancakes." She flips the coin again and it comes up Foxy. "Pancakes!"

"I never agreed to that," you grumble. But you go to the kitchen and start mixing the batter. It's only after she leaves for school that you remember Foxy's head is on both sides of the coin.

➤ TURN TO PAGE 86

Home again. You stop in the kitchen and wash your hands vigorously under the hottest water you can stand for two minutes, and they still don't feel clean. This last night has left a mark on you that you don't think will ever come out.

You head to your daughter's room and run into her in the hall, already dressed for school. Coppelia has bags under her eyes. You look at each other for a moment and then she wraps you in a tight hug.

"Are you okay?" she whispers. Her voice trembles.

"I'm alive." You laugh, but neither of you finds it funny. "Are *you* okay? Why are you up so early?"

"I didn't sleep well." The two of you walk back to the kitchen together. She holds on to your arm. "Someone called last night. Looking for you."

"Who? When?"

"She didn't say. She called a minute after you left, hoping to catch you."

"Did she leave a message?"

"She said she would and then she hung up. There wasn't a very good connection."

"Huh. If it's important she'll call back."

You don't feel up to making breakfast and Coppelia doesn't seem up to eating much, so you pour two bowls of sugary cereal.

"I'm glad you're home," she says.

"Me too."

"Can't I skip school? I want to hang out with you."

You're tempted, but she needs to go to class. That's what kids do, right? Just like you have to work.

➤ TURN TO PAGE 236

"I don't think so. Not today, sweetie. I need to sleep, anyway."

"Go ahead. I just want to be around you."

"Staring at me while I sleep? Sounds creepy." You wink and you both laugh. And just like that, whatever has been haunting you lifts and memories of the awful night fade away.

"Tell you what. You can stay home if you tidy your room. It's getting to be a mess, and I'm done cleaning up after other people."

"No deal."

You smirk. *Thought so.*

"So, bring me any souvenirs?" she asks as she ties her shoes.

"I did find a couple of things lying around."

An image of the large bloody puddle pops into your mind. Your breakfast starts to come back up, but you swallow it down. It leaves a bad taste in your mouth.

"Dad? What's wrong?"

"Tonight was . . . a lot. I'll tell you about it later." Never. "Here's your prize for being Daughter of the Month . . ."

You reach into your bag.

➤ IF YOU HAVE THE <u>GOLD RING</u> AND WANT TO HAND IT TO HER,
   TURN TO PAGE 237

➤ IF YOU HAVE <u>MR. CUPCAKE</u> AND WANT TO HAND IT TO HER,
   TURN TO PAGE 238

➤ IF YOU HAVE THE <u>WATER PISTOL</u> AND WANT TO HAND IT TO HER,
   TURN TO PAGE 239

➤ IF YOU FLASH HER A THUMBS-UP AND SEND HER OFF TO SCHOOL,
   TURN TO PAGE 121

She inspects the gold ring.

"Don't bite down on it," you say hurriedly. "I think it's real gold."

She slips the ring on her right hand. It fits her perfectly.

She smiles. "Am I invisible now?"

You look around in confusion. "Pel? Where did you go? I can hear you, but I can't see you."

She pulls the ring off.

"Oh, there you are!" You grin. Just like when she was a year old and you used to play peekaboo together. She would laugh and laugh. Oh, to be young enough to believe that just because you can't see someone, they can't see you, either.

"Thank you for my preciousssss," she says.

"I never should have let you read *The Lord of the Rings*," you say.

"Let me? Like you could have stopped me. You give me everything I want." She tilts her head. "Almost everything . . ."

"Go to school!" You point to the door and she shrugs.

"I had to try." She puts the ring on again. You blink and she's gone. This time for real.

What? You check the time and see an hour has passed. You must have fallen asleep right there at the table as she was leaving.

You crawl off to bed, but now that you're lying there, you have a hard time falling asleep.

➤ REMOVE THE <u>GOLD RING</u> FROM YOUR INVENTORY AND TURN TO PAGE 121

She inspects the toy cupcake.

"Don't bite down on it," you say. "It's not a real cupcake."

She turns it from side to side. "It's . . . cute?"

"Was that a question mark?" you ask.

"I think so?" She squints at Mr. Cupcake. "I mean, it's goofy, so I kind of like it. Doesn't that chicken carry this around?"

"Chica."

"Right. Don't you think it's messed up that chicken wings are on the menu when one of the stars of the restaurant is a giant chicken?"

You sigh. "They're called Chica's Hot Wings, too. That's above my pay grade."

She stows Mr. Cupcake in her backpack. "Thanks, Daddy. I'm gonna show this to my friends at school. I'll see you later."

"Be good and have a good day!"

As tired as you are, it takes you a while to fall asleep. So you're annoyed when the phone rings a couple of hours later.

You pick up the handset and bark, "What?"

"Are you Coppelia's father?" a woman asks.

You sit up in bed. "Yes. Is she all right?"

"We were hoping you could tell us. She didn't show up for school this morning."

"Was she on the bus?"

"No one has seen her since yesterday afternoon."

You drop the phone and run outside to the bus stop on the corner. You find Coppelia's backpack there, torn to shreds, her books and papers scattered and blowing in the wind.

GAME OVER

➤ TO START FROM THE BEGINNING, TURN TO PAGE 2
➤ TO RESTART THIS SCENE, TURN TO PAGE 235

She spins the water pistol around her finger like a Wild West gun-slinger and then points it at your chest.

"'You've got to ask yourself one question: Do I feel lucky? Well, do you, punk?'"

"This was a mistake. Gimme." You reach out to take back the toy gun.

"Oh, you want it?"

"Yes, let me have it."

"Okay!" She squeezes the trigger and water squirts you in the face. Her peals of laughter fill the kitchen.

"Thanks." You wipe the water from your face and watch her laughing.

"You asked for it," she says.

"I sure did."

She starts to put the water pistol in her backpack.

"Nope!" you say.

"Aw. I wasn't going to use it." She pulls the water pistol out sadly.

"Then why bring it?"

"It makes me feel safer," she says.

"It shoots water."

"The Wicked Witch of the West has been bullying me at school lately, and I really think this would help me manage that situation."

"You are not going to murder the Wicked Witch of the West. Leave it here. It'll be waiting for you after school."

"What a world." She puts the toy down on the coffee table. "What about you?"

"I'll be here, too."

She smiles. "Good!"

She leaves and you head to bed. When you close your eyes, all you see are the horrors of the night. Then you feel your damp hair and you laugh and fall asleep.

➤ REMOVE THE <u>WATER PISTOL</u> FROM YOUR INVENTORY AND
TURN TO PAGE 121

When you get home, you head straight for your daughter's room, but she isn't there. Shaking with fear, you call out for her and search the house.

"Coppelia! Coppelia!"

"In here!" Her voice is muffled, but it sounds like it's coming from your bedroom. You rush upstairs and find her sitting on your messy bed in her pajamas.

"Pel!" You rush to her side and grab her in a tight embrace.

"Ow. What's wrong?"

"I was worried when you weren't in your room. What are you doing in here?"

She yawns. "I missed you, Daddy."

"I missed you, too, kiddo. Any reason?"

"Because you weren't here. Duh."

You roll your eyes. You lie next to her and stare up at the ceiling while she snuggles against you.

This is nice, you think. Coppelia used to do this all the time when she was little, but you know these days are numbered. Eventually, probably sooner than you like, she won't even want to talk to you. You'll miss all those sleepless nights with her tossing and turning, sticking her feet in your face, lying on your arm until it's numb.

So you'd better enjoy it while you can.

The next thing you know, Coppelia is kissing you good-bye on the cheek. She is dressed for school and holding a Pop-Tart in one hand, her backpack in the other.

"I'm leaving," she says. "Daddy, can you stay home from work tonight?"

"I can't," you mumble, already falling back to sleep. "Just one last night . . ."

➤ TURN TO PAGE 158

You don't remember the drive home or falling asleep on the couch, but you wake up and Coppelia is sitting at the end of the couch, your feet in her lap, while she plays a video game.

"What . . . What time is it?" You struggle to sit up.

"Dad! You messed up my high score." She keeps operating the controller. "It's eleven."

"Uh. Eleven p.m.?" It's pouring and gray outside the window, but it's clearly daytime. "Shouldn't you be in school?"

"You said I could stay home today."

"I did?" You rub your bleary eyes. "I don't remember that."

"You crashed pretty hard when you got home from work." You hear a digitized crashing sound from the TV as the pink car collides head-on with a purple car. She shakes her fist. "Purple car!"

She sets the controller down and shifts to face you. "How does it feel?"

"Huh?"

"Being done with that job!"

You frown.

"Dad. No. You're done, right? You quit?"

"I . . . might need to go back tonight. I left some unfinished business."

"Let someone else finish it! You were wrecked when you came home. This week almost killed you. Just put it all behind you. I'll eat PB&Js if you're worried about the money."

Coppelia presses her hands together. *"Please."*

This is where you need to be right now, but you still lie awake at night worrying about how long you can keep her safe.

THE END.

➤ IF YOU SIGN UP FOR OVERTIME, TURN TO PAGE 201

You aren't making any progress in these vents and you don't have much time. You slide the mobile phone from the back of your belt and scroll through the contacts. You need to get to the stage, so you dial the Dining Area and strain your ears to listen.

There! The ringing phone is very distant and barely audible—you've really gotten turned around in here. But now you have a sonic beacon leading you in the right direction. You keep the phone line open and follow the sound through the corridors until it's loud and clear. You spot an exit up ahead and are both relieved and concerned that someone else has already torn off the metal ventilation cover and crumpled it up like a discarded candy wrapper.

At this point, you don't care if there's an animatronic waiting for you—you are done with these vents. You disconnect the call and clamber out of there.

You seem to be all alone in the Dining Area, even though the ringing phone should have attracted the animatronics. You worry that you're already too late. You hurry to the hatch for the crawlspace and wriggle inside.

The switchbox for the charging platform has cables snaking out of it, more than there should be. There are six small metal switches, alternating in the "up" and "down" positions. You have no idea what you're looking at. It's time to dial a friend.

➤ CALL DAVE THE MAINTENANCE GUY ON PAGE 243

"Ralph." Dave yawns. "This is becoming a habit. How did you get my home number, anyway?"

"That's not important," you say. "So . . . I'm in the crawlspace under the stage. There are six switches, and I think someone's been messing with them."

"What?" Dave sighs. "I'm coming over. But I'd better get overtime for this, or it's coming out of your pay."

"No!" you say. *I don't want you to die.* "You shouldn't have to come here in the middle of the night. Can't you just talk me through it?"

"Do the switches match the positions in the diagram taped to the power relay?"

You look around but you don't see any such diagram, and you tell him so.

"All right, what positions are they in?" he asks.

"The first one is up, the second is down. Then up, down, up, and down."

Dave swears. "You gotta fix this, Ralph. There's no telling what will happen to the animatronics if they get too much or too little power. It could cause all sorts of malfunctions, damage their batteries . . ."

"Send them on a murderous rampage?"

Dave is quiet. "Not funny, Ralph."

"Sorry."

"Here's the correct configuration. You ready? You might want to put on some rubber gloves for this."

You don't see those, either, but you're sure it'll be all right. Dave tells you to flip the first three switches up, the next two down, and leave the last one in the middle. Sparks fly and you get a little jolt as you follow his instructions.

➤ TURN TO PAGE 244

"That should do it," Dave says. "Hey, I thought you quit. Wasn't your last shift last night?"

"I just had some unfinished business," you say. "This is my final night at Freddy's."

"Well, it's been nice working with you. Good luck. And lose this number." *Click.*

"Thanks, Dave. I'll miss you, too."

You study the power relay, waiting for something to happen. Then you realize this isn't going to change anything: You just put the switches back how they're supposed to be, but the animatronics are already powered up. The only way to stop them now is to overload them the way Dave said you shouldn't, or drain the excess charge from their batteries. How do you do that?

You doubt Dave will tell you how to sabotage the animatronics, if he even takes another call from you, so now you're on your own.

➤ IF YOU FLIP ALL THE SWITCHES UP, TURN TO PAGE 208

➤ IF YOU FLIP ALL THE SWITCHES DOWN, TURN TO PAGE 209

ABOUT THE AUTHORS

SCOTT CAWTHON is the author of the bestselling video game series *Five Nights at Freddy's*, and while he is a game designer by trade, he is first and foremost a storyteller at heart. He is a graduate of The Art Institute of Houston and lives in Texas with his family.

E. C. MYERS was assembled in the United States from Korean and German parts and raised by a single mother and the public library in Yonkers, New York. He won the Andre Norton Nebula Award for his first novel, *Fair Coin* (2012), and is the author of *The Silence of Six* and the RWBY young adult books, including *After the Fall* (2019), *Fairy Tales of Remnant* (2020), and *Roman Holiday* (2021). His short fiction has been published in various anthologies, including *Tasting Light: Ten Science Fiction Stories to Rewire Your Perceptions*, *Mother of Invention*, and *A Thousand Beginnings and Endings*. He has also written for several serialized podcasts, including *The Sounds of Nightmares* (from the world of *Little Nightmares*) and *Orphan Black: The Next Chapter*.

NOTES

A DEADLY SECRET IS LURKING AT THE HEART OF FREDDY FAZBEAR'S PIZZA...

Unravel the twisted mysteries behind the bestselling horror video games and the *New York Times* bestselling series.

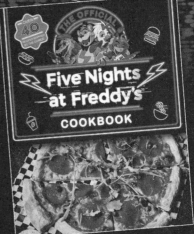